MUSIC FROM THE HEART

"I think I . . . ought to . . . go away," Ilouka managed to say.

The Earl smiled again. "Do you really think I would let you do that?" he asked.

Ilouka stared at him as if she could not believe what he was saying. Then as she was trying to find words he put his fingers under her chin and turned her face up to his. Then, incredibly, so that she could hardly believe what was happening, his lips came down on hers.

Ilouka had never been kissed and she had no idea that a man's lips could make her feel as if she was his captive, and it was impossible to try to escape. When she told herself that she must struggle, she felt as if a streak of lightning swept through her body.

It was the strange ecstasy she had felt when she was dancing that seemed to come from some music within her heart and which she felt must be in the Earl's heart too, and that they listened to it together. . . .

Bantam Books by Barbara Cartland
Ask your bookseller for the books you have missed

Barbara Cartland's Library of Love Series
BEYOND THE ROCKS

A NEW SERVICE FOR
BARBARA CARTLAND READERS

Now you can have the latest Barbara Cartland romances delivered to your home automatically each month. For further information on this new reader service, contact the Direct Response Department, Bantam Books, 666 Fifth Avenue, New York, N.Y. 10103. Phone (212) 765-6500.

Music
from the Heart

Barbara Cartland

BANTAM BOOKS

TORONTO · NEW YORK · LONDON · SYDNEY

MUSIC FROM THE HEART
A Bantam Book / May 1982

ISBN 0-553-22513-8

Published simultaneously in the United States and Canada

*Bantam Books are published by Bantam Books, Inc. Its trade-
mark, consisting of the words "Bantam Books" and the por-
trayal of a rooster, is Registered in U.S. Patent and Trademark
Office and in other countries. Marca Registrada. Bantam
Books, Inc., 666 Fifth Avenue, New York, New York 10103.*

PRINTED IN THE UNITED STATES OF AMERICA

0 9 8 7 6 5 4 3 2 1

Author's Note

William IV and his prim little German wife, Queen Adelaide, raised the moral standard of England, which had fallen to a very low level during the raffish, extravagant reign of George IV.

Unfortunately, propriety at Court also meant boredom and evenings when the Gentlemen-in-Waiting yawned themselves to bed. In consequence, the parties and entertainments which the late Monarch had enjoyed took place in the private houses of noblemen.

Madame Vestris scandalised and delighted London during the Regency by appearing on the stage dressed in breeches. She continued to play male parts during the reigns of William IV and Queen Victoria and made a great success of the Royal Olympic Theatre.

Before the Season opened on January 3, 1831, Madame began to alter theatre practice in Britain. She paid salaries in advance and had a proper regulation of working hours and breaks.

Within an hour of the opening of the Season, Madame progressed another innovation—the design of a setting exclusively related to the matter of the play!

She ran the Royal Olympic Theatre until 1839, appeared in New York at the Park Theatre, went on to manage the Theatre Royal Convent Garden, and to appear at the Haymarket and several other Theatres. She received an ovation at the Lyceum in 1854 at her final performance and died the following year.

Madame Vestris was undoubtedly one of the most fascinating personalities of the stage, and she made theatrical history as a Manageress and an Innovator.

Chapter One
1831

Sir James Armstrong read the letter he held in his hand, and when he had finished there was a smile of satisfaction on his face.

He looked across the breakfast-table at his wife and said:

"Denton is coming. I thought he would not be able to resist a Steeple-Chase!"

Before Lady Armstrong could reply, her step-daughter, Muriel, gave a cry of delight.

"Denton has really accepted, Papa?" she asked. "That is wonderful!"

"I thought it would please you," Sir James said.

"I am thrilled!" Muriel Armstrong replied. "He said he wanted to see me again."

She looked down a little coyly, then as she raised her eyes she looked at her step-sister and the expression on her face changed.

"I am not having Ilouka here," she said in a very different tone of voice.

Her father looked at his wife in surprise, raising his eye-brows, and there was an expression of concern on Lady Armstrong's beautiful face.

Ever since she had married for the second time, she

had been upset by the animosity with which her step-child regarded her daughter by her previous marriage.

It was creating an atmosphere of tension in the house, which she very much deprecated.

"Ilouka will have to go away!" Muriel said insistently. "I will not have her spoiling my chance of attracting Lord Denton as she did with Frederick Holder."

"That was not my fault," Ilouka said quickly. "I promise you it was not."

Her voice was soft and musical, very different from her step-sister's aggressive tone.

There was a frown between Sir James's eyes as he said slowly:

"I know my sister Agatha would be only too pleased to have Ilouka to stay."

"Then that is where she must go," Muriel said quickly.

Ilouka parted her lips as if to protest, but before she could speak she caught her mother's warning glance and the words died on her lips.

She knew her mother was pleading with her to be silent, and it was only when they had left the Breakfast-Room and mother and daughter walked up the stairs together that each knew without words what the other was thinking.

Lady Armstrong went into the Sitting-Room which led off her bedroom and as Ilouka closed the door she said pleadingly:

"Oh, please, Mama, I cannot go to stay with Mrs. Adolphus again. You know how terrible it was the last time. She never stopped saying nasty things about you in a rather subtle manner."

Lady Armstrong sighed.

"I am afraid your step-father's relations did not approve of his marrying a penniless widow who they thought would be too old to give him a son, or indeed any more children."

"How can they be so unkind when Step-Papa is so happy, if it were not for Muriel?"

"Yes, I know, dearest," Lady Armstrong agreed in a soft voice. "but perhaps she will marry Lord Denton, and then there will be no further problems. But you know as well as I do that if you are here when he arrives, you will spoil her chances."

Both mother and daughter were silent, knowing that Ilouka could not help attracting men, and it was only too true that when she was there Muriel had no chance of holding the attention of a man for long.

Muriel was in fact quite a good-looking girl, with clear skin and brown hair complemented by brown eyes which could, when she wanted something, be soft and appealing, but were as hard as iron if she was crossed.

It seemed from her point of view singularly unfair that her father, after years of apparently being content to be a widower pursued by a great number of attractive women, had fallen in love with the widow of a near neighbour.

When Colonel Compton had died, his wife was so miserable and bereft without him that it would not have occurred to her as possible that she should marry again.

But the Colonel, who had been a distinguished soldier and had, as someone had once said, "more charm in his little finger than most men have in the whole of their bodies," had never been a thrifty man.

His wife discovered a multitude of debts which she thought despairingly would take her years to pay off, and it meant that she and her daughter, Ilouka, would have to skimp and save every penny.

Of course there could be no new gowns, and certainly no London Season where Ilouka would shine as her mother had hoped for her in the Social World that she had known as a girl.

She was not at all interested in Sir James Armstrong, who, having called to commiserate with her on her bereavement, came again and again until it was quite obvious that he was courting her.

However, it was impossible not to realise how very different life would be if she became his wife.

His impressive country house with a large Estate was a focal point in the County for those who liked to be invited to his luncheons and dinner-parties.

They also enjoyed the garden-parties he gave in the summer and the two Hunt Balls which always took place at The Towers in the winter.

It was knowing the difference it would make to Ilouka which persuaded Mrs. Compton finally to accept Sir James's proposal, after he had grown more ardent and more insistent week by week and day by day.

Although she knew that nobody could ever take the place of her husband in her heart, she in fact grew very fond of Sir James.

Being a very feminine person, she longed once more to be protected and looked after and to feel that the burden of unpaid debts that her husband had left her, together with her memories of him, would no longer feel as if it was crushing her.

Finally, after a year of mourning, she allowed Sir James to announce their wedding after it had taken place very quietly and with nobody there except two of his closest friends.

When they came back from their honeymoon, the new Lady Armstrong looked not only radiant but exceedingly beautiful in expensive gowns such as she had never owned before, and with jewellery with which Sir James expressed his love more eloquently than he could put into words.

Ilouka joined her at The Towers, and then unfortunately a month later Muriel, Sir James's only child by his first marriage, also arrived.

It was impossible for anyone not to realise the contrast between the two girls, although they were almost the same age.

Ilouka was lovely with a beauty which owed a lot to her Hungarian grandmother, as did the colour of her hair.

· The very soft, dark red that the Hungarians all through the centuries have made their own was complemented by two enormous eyes, which dominated her face and which were green flecked with gold.

She was small and delicately made, and it was impossible for a man having once looked at her not to look again, and, unfortunately as far as Muriel was concerned, to forget there was any other woman in the room.

In some ways she resembled her mother, but it was her father who had told her stories of his grandmother after whom she had been named.

She had been a famous beauty in Hungary, and she run away with an obscure, unimportant young English Diplomat named Compton when it was all arranged that she should marry a rich aristocrat.

As a child Ilouka wanted to hear the story over and over again, and her father had said:

"Your name means: 'She who gives life,' and although I knew her only when she was very old, my grandmother still seemed to give life to everybody round her. It was nothing she specially did or said, it was just that she inspired people and gave them a vibration of the life-force just by being herself."

"How did she do that, Papa?" Ilouka had asked.

Her father had laughed and said that when she grew up she would have to read books on Hungary and visit the country to understand what he meant.

As Mrs. Compton watched her daughter grow up and become more and more beautiful every day and having, she thought, a quality about her which English girls did not possess, she realised it was unlikely that the more stolid and prosaic County people would appreciate the rare and un-English quality about her.

"We must see that she is presented to the King and Queen," she had said to her husband.

"I agree," he answered, "but God knows where the money is going to come from!"

Sir James was, of course, able to find the money, but unfortunately there was Muriel like a stumbling-block between Ilouka and her mother's ambitions.

"One cannot blame Muriel," Lady Armstrong said now with a sigh, "when you turn the head of every young man who comes to the house."

"I do not want them!" Ilouka replied. "As you know, Mama, most of them are dull and unimaginative and I could no more marry any of them than fly to the moon."

"I know, darling, but as things are, how are you to meet the right sort of man unless I can take you to London for a Season, and that would mean that Muriel would have to come too."

Ilouka gave a little cry.

"I could not bear it, Mama! She is so terribly jealous, and because she hates me it makes me feel not only unhappy but nervous and ill-at-ease."

She gave a little laugh but there was no humour in it as she said:

"In fact, I am afraid even to speak to a man if she is present."

Lady Armstrong knew without her adding it that any man present would want to speak to Ilouka.

Looking at her daughter now, she thought as she had so often thought before that it was not only her beauty that was so arresting, but the fact that there was something ethereal and almost supernatural about her.

"She is like a fairy-child," she had once said to Colonel Compton, and he had replied:

"Seeing how much we love each other and how happy we are together, my darling, is it surprising that we have produced something unusual who might actually have come out of a fairy-tale?"

He himself was very handsome, and wherever they went they were stared at.

It was unfortunate from their point of view that because of limited resources they were restricted to their small Manor House in Oxfordshire and it was only occasionally that they could afford a brief visit to London.

Mrs. Compton wanted so much more for her daughter, but now, when as Lady Armstrong she could afford it, there was Muriel.

"If I am to go away," Ilouka asked, "why should I have to stay with Mrs. Adolphus?"

Her mother made a helpless little gesture with her hands.

"She is the only member of your step-father's family who is willing to do exactly as he asks," she replied, "and I think too, although he would not admit it, he feels rather ashamed of having to send you away. He therefore wishes to send you where nobody would talk about it and in consequence disparage Muriel."

Ilouka drew in her breath but did not reply, and after a moment her mother went on:

"Actually your step-father is very fond of you, Ilouka dearest, but naturally his first thought must be for his own child, and you know as well as I do that Muriel has always resented him marrying again."

"How can she be so selfish, Mama, when you know how happy you have made Step-Papa? He loves you with all his heart."

"Yes, I know," Lady Armstrong agreed. "At the same time, he has a great sense of family, and he must do what is right and best for Muriel."

Ilouka pressed her soft lips together in case she should say anything to hurt her mother, but she was thinking how they both knew that Muriel had raged at her father furiously when she first learnt that he had married again.

Unfortunately, she had also written a lot of extremely derogatory and unkind letters, which Sir James very foolishly had shown to his wife after he had married her.

He had done so not to distress her but because he thought it was right that she should know the problems awaiting them both when their honeymoon was over.

Lady Armstrong had tried by every means in her power to make Muriel like her, and she might have succeeded if Muriel had not been eaten up with jealousy, spite, and malice from the moment she had first set eyes on Ilouka.

She had deliberately set out on what amounted to a

campaign of spite against Ilouka and where possible to drive a wedge between her father and his new wife.

There she was completely unsuccessful, although she often made Lady Armstrong very unhappy.

But where Ilouka was concerned she managed to make her life a series of petty insults and slights that grew worse every day that they were in the same house together.

"It will be a relief, Mama, to go away," Ilouka said now. "At the same time, please, please do not let me stay away very long."

"You know, dearest, I have planned to present you at a 'Drawing-Room' in May," Lady Armstrong replied, "and your step-father wishes me to present Muriel at the same time. But now I cannot help feeling that it would be impossible to enjoy a London Season together."

"I do not mind missing the Season," Ilouka said, "but I do mind being away from you, especially with Mrs. Adolphus."

Lady Armstrong sighed.

She was well aware that her husband's sister hated her because she had set her heart on her brother marrying again and having several sons.

She was a demanding, elderly woman who her enemies said had driven her husband into the grave and then had transferred her ambitions to her only brother.

She lived in a bleak, ugly house in Bedfordshire, where the flatness of the countryside seemed somehow to echo the deadly boredom of the neighbourhood and of Mrs. Adolphus's household in particular.

The servants were old and crotchety and resented visitors because they made extra work.

The food was plain and dull, and even the horses which Ilouka was allowed to ride were slow and unspirited.

With her Hungarian blood she had all the talents that had made her great-grandmother so outstanding.

A magnificent rider, she could master any horse, however wild and unruly, and she was also extremely musical and with her fairy-like figure could dance in a way that made her father say once:

"We must put Ilouka on the stage at Covent Garden, and the money she obtains in 'Benefits' will keep us in comfort in our old age!"

His wife had protested laughingly.

"How can you say anything so outrageous, darling? For goodness' sake, do not put such ideas into Ilouka's head!"

"I was not serious," Colonel Compton had laughed.

Nevertheless, he would make Ilouka dance for him while her mother played the piano.

In the music was the wild dance of the Hungarian gypsies, and Ilouka would dance as if her feet never touched the ground and she flowed with a grace and an abandon that came from her instinct and not from anything she had ever seen.

"I tell you what I will do," Lady Armstrong said now, after a pause while she had been considering what her daughter had said. "You must go to Agatha before Lord Denton arrives, but I will write to your father's sister who lives not far away in Huntingdon and ask her if she will take you for a short while."

Ilouka's face lit up.

"I would like that," she said. "Aunt Alice is a sweet person, and I love her children."

"I know, dearest, but you do realise they are very poor, and although we could not insult them by offering money, even one extra would strain their resources even more than they are strained already."

As she spoke Lady Armstrong was thinking of how difficult it had been for her and Ilouka after her husband died.

"You know I understand," Ilouka said, "and perhaps you could give me some money to buy presents for the children; not toys or games which are really useless, but dresses for the little girls and perhaps a coat for each of the boys."

"Of course I will do that," her mother replied. "At

the same time, you will have to be very, very careful
not to let them feel it is an act of charity."

"Leave it to me, Mama. You know I would not do
anything to hurt Aunt Alice."

"Then I will write to her at once."

"I suppose I could not go there first, and not to Mrs.
Adolphus?"

Lady Armstrong shook her head.

"Your step-father thinks his sister is a delightful person."

"She always is, to him."

"It is only that she dislikes me, and in consequence
you," her mother went on.

"Yes, I know," Ilouka said, "but it means that she will
find fault every moment of the day, and will keep on
telling me over and over again what wonderful chances
her brother missed when he married you."

Lady Armstrong laughed.

"You will just have to remember that neither he nor I
are complaining."

"I know, Mama, but she goes on and on, almost as if
Step-Papa picked you up from the gutter, or you trapped
him into marriage when he was least expecting it!"

Lady Armstrong laughed again, remembering how
Sir James had pleaded with her and begged her to
marry him so humbly that now in retrospect it seemed
almost incredible how abject he had been at the time.

But she was in fact growing more fond of him all the
time that they were together, and she prayed that for all
their sakes Muriel would get married soon.

Then as far as she was concerned she could enjoy
having a husband who adored her and who was prepared to give her all the money she needed for herself
and her daughter.

At the same time, Sir James had his little meannesses,
and one of these was that he did not like to send his
own horses on long distances and he resented hiring
conveyances when his stable was full.

"Ilouka will leave for your sister's early the day after
tomorrow," Lady Armstrong said. "If she starts early in

the morning, she will only have to stay for one night on the way, and you know I do not like her staying at Posting-Inns, even with a maid to look after her."

There was silence while both Sir James and his wife were thinking that Lord Denton was unlikely to arrive before tea-time, and by that time Ilouka would be far away.

Lady Armstrong then said pleadingly:

"You will send her in a carriage, James?"

"That is impossible," Sir James replied. "I need all the coachmen and the grooms here to help with the Steeple-Chase, and it is also too far for our best horses."

Lady Armstrong stiffened. Then she asked:

"Then how are you suggesting that Ilouka should get to your sister's house?"

"She can go by Stage-Coach," Sir James replied. "After all, it will hardly be a new experience for her."

This was true, because before Lady Armstrong married Sir James she had during her widowhood been obliged to dispose of her horses, and she and Ilouka had therefore had no option but to travel by Stage-Coach.

There was a little silence. Then Lady Armstrong said:

"I suppose if she is with Hannah she will be all right."

"Of course she will be all right," Sir James said sharply, "and very much safer than if she travelled by Post-Chaise, which is the only alternative."

"The Stage-Coaches are so slow," Lady Armstrong said, "and they do not always stop at the best Inns."

"I imagine, as it is a cross-country journey, there will not be much choice," Sir James replied drily.

Lady Armstrong was perturbed. At the same time, she knew that her husband would have made up his mind, and she thought that to plead with him to change it would be a mistake and might affect Ilouka.

He had already said that she should have a Season in London, and although they were both well aware that it would be difficult because of Muriel, so far he had not

renounced his intention of opening his London House
to give a Ball for both the girls.

Lady Armstrong was quite certain that behind her
back Muriel was trying by every means she could to
have Ilouka excluded.

But she was also confident that her husband would
be too loyal to her to agree to what his daughter
suggested.

At the same time, it would be a mistake to upset him
in any way at this particular moment, and she could
only pray more fervently than she was doing already
that Muriel would marry Lord Denton, and Ilouka
could then enjoy a Season alone.

Aloud she said:

"I will see that Ilouka is ready and that Hannah goes
with her. Will you order a carriage to convey them to
the cross-roads? And please ask whoever goes with
them to see that she has a comfortable seat and to tip
the Guard so that he will look after her."

"You know I will do that," Sir James said.

Then he put his hand on his wife's shoulder as he
said:

"I am sorry to send Ilouka away, my darling, if it
upsets you. At the same time, Denton is quite a catch,
and I would welcome him as a son-in-law."

The tone of voice in which he spoke said far more
than the words he used, and Lady Armstrong quickly
put her hand over his as she said:

"You know, dearest, that I want Muriel's happiness
just as I want yours."

Sir James bent his head to kiss her cheek and said no
more, but Lady Armstrong knew by the expression in
his eyes before he left the room how much he loved
her.

At the same time, she could not help worrying about
Ilouka.

Then she told herself that there was actually nothing
to worry about except that her daughter would be
exceedingly bored on the long journey across country.

The Stage-Coach would not be packed with dashing young men who might be beguiled by her beauty, but with farmers' wives journeying to a market-town, commercial travellers intent on what they could sell, and perhaps a few farm-boys returning home after taking a horse to sell at a Fair or driving a herd of cows to a new purchaser.

'And who could look after Ilouka more effectively than Hannah?' she thought with a smile.

Hannah had been their only maid after the Colonel's death, because they had been unable to afford any more servants.

She was a strict Presbyterian who thought the whole world was a wicked place filled with people who in her own words were "up to no good!"

Even the tradesmen who came to the Manor had been afraid of Hannah, and Lady Armstrong knew that any man who even attempted to talk to Ilouka without an introduction would be annihilated by Hannah's eyes before the first word had left his lips.

"I am afraid it will be a rather long and boring journey for you, Hannah," she said to the old maid in her sweet manner which every servant found irresistible.

"Duty is duty, M'Lady," Hannah replied, "and the Good Lord never said anything about it being a pleasure!"

"I know Miss Ilouka will be quite safe with you," Lady Armstrong went on.

"You can be sure of that, M'Lady."

"All the same," Lady Armstrong continued as if she spoke to herself, "I wish the Master could have spared a coach to take you to Bedfordshire."

Hannah's lips tightened, making her look very formidable.

Now that she was nearing seventy, the lines on her face were deeply ingrained, and when she was angry, as an impertinent footman once said, "She looks like an old gargoyle!"

Hannah had never really approved of Sir James from the time he came courting her mistress.

At the same time, she definitely appreciated the comforts of their new home, but she deeply resented it if "her ladies," as she thought of them in her mind, were insulted in any way.

"I am not so sorry for myself having to travel in the Stage-Coach," Ilouka said to her mother when they were alone, "but for the other travellers who will have to put up with Hannah! I cannot tell you, Mama, how intimidating she can be."

"I have seen her," Lady Armstrong replied, laughing.

The eyes of both mother and daughter twinkled at each other as they envisaged how Hannah, sitting bolt upright, would by her very presence seem to cast a gloom over the other occupants of the Stage-Coach.

Those who might have been talking gaily and vociferously before would lapse into an uneasy silence, and any man who dared to whistle beneath his breath would receive such a look of disapproval that he would hastily shut his eyes and pretend to go to sleep.

The cards with which men wiled away a long journey were frowned upon by Hannah to a point where a game lost its interest, and small children who otherwise might have been obstreperous hid their heads shyly against their mothers.

"I shall be perfectly all right," Ilouka siad. "Do not worry about me on the journey, Mama, but only when I reach Stone House, which is appropriately named!"

Both mother and daughter laughed, then Lady Armstrong said:

"Oh, dear, I wish worthy people were not always so dismal and dreary about it. I know Agatha Adolphus does a great deal of good one way and another, but I am sure as soon as she has bestowed her charity upon them it makes those who receive it long to go out and do something really wicked."

Ilouka put her arm round her mother's neck and kissed her.

"I love you, Mama! You always understand, and if

after I have stayed with Mrs. Adolphus I do something really wicked, you must not blame me."

Lady Armstrong gave a little cry.

"Oh, Ilouka, I should not have said that, and please, darling, just do all the things I should want you to do in your usual adorable manner. Then perhaps even Agatha Adolphus will not seem so formidable."

"She will!" Ilouka said lightly. "She is like the Rock of Gilbraltar, and nothing, neither tempest nor earthquake, will change her, and certainly I will not."

They laughed again, but when the next morning Ilouka was ready to leave, she held on tightly to her mother.

"I love you, Mama!" she said. "I will hate being away from you."

"I shall miss you too, dearest," Lady Armstrong replied, "but there is nothing else either of us can do."

"Nothing," Ilouka agreed.

She would not upset her mother by telling her that last night when they had gone up to bed together Muriel had said to her:

"Surely there must be some men in Bedfordshire and you ought to be able to get your hands on one of them."

Ilouka had not replied and Muriel had gone on spitefully:

"You have certainly tried hard enough to encourage some idiots to propose to you, and now when they do so you only have to say 'yes.'"

As if she goaded Ilouka into a reply she said unwisely:

"I do not wish to marry anybody until I can find somebody I can love."

"That sounds very high and mighty," Muriel sneered, "and of course it will be very easy for you to fall in love with a man if he has a lot of money like my father!"

Ilouka stiffened, and Muriel went on:

"It was very convenient, was it not, your mother sitting wistfully on the door-step, so to speak, and looking so pathetic in a cheap black gown because she could not afford anything better."

The angry, spiteful note in Muriel's voice seemed to be reflected in her face, and Ilouka thought that when she spoke like that she looked ugly and it was unlikely that any man unless he was blind would want to marry her.

Because she would not demean herself to answer anything so untrue or so unkind, she merely said as they reached her bedroom door:

"Good-night, Muriel. You may not believe this, but I want you to be happy, and I hope and pray that Lord Denton will give it to you."

She did not wait for Muriel's answer, which she was certain would be vindictive, but went into her own room and shut the door.

Only when she was alone did she feel as if she was trembling, as she always did when she heard her mother being abused.

After her father's death, her mother had thought it impossible for any man ever to mean anything to her, and she had said over and over again:

"Your father and I were so happy, so ideally, perfectly happy! All I want now is to die so that I can be with him."

Ilouka had looked at her in horror.

"You must not say such things, Mama. It is very selfish. After all, if you die I shall be all alone in the world, and you know I could not live without you."

Mrs. Compton had put her arms round her daughter and held her close.

"You are right, darling, I was being selfish. But I miss your Papa so much that I feel that the world has come to an end, because he is no longer with me."

However, for her daughter's sake, Mrs. Compton made a great effort.

She cried herself to sleep every night when whe was alone in her own room, but in the day-time she tried to smile and to take an interest in what Ilouka was doing.

They went for long walks and talked of many things,

both aware that while they did not mention it, Colonel Compton's name was uppermost in their minds.

Then gradually, as the first agony of grief passed and Sir James started to call, Mrs. Compton began to stop making excuses not to see him.

"It will do you good, Mama, to talk to Sir James," Ilouka would say. "Now tidy your hair and go down and make yourself pleasant to him."

"Oh, must I, Ilouka? I do not want to," Mrs. Compton would plead.

"He has brought us a huge basket of peaches from his greenhouses, and some grapes," Ilouka would reply, "and even if you do not eat them, Mama, Hannah and I would find them a pleasant change from semolina pudding."

Because she felt too exhausted to argue, Mrs. Compton would do as her daughter suggested.

It was impossible to explain to Muriel that she had no wish to trap anybody or to put them in her beloved husband's place.

But now, as Ilouka knew, they were happy, very happy, except for Muriel.

'I would go and stay with the Devil himself,' she thought, 'if it gave Muriel the chance to marry and go away!'

At the same time, she faced the fact that even if Muriel got engaged it might be the conventional long engagement.

That would mean that she would have to stay in hiding until the ring was actually on Muriel's finger and her fiancé could not change his mind at the last moment.

It was true that Ilouka had never made the slightest effort to attract any man's attention, but it was also true that she had not had much opportunity.

Nevertheless, her father's friends had looked at her with astonishment when they came to the Manor, and even when she was a School-girl with her long hair flowing over her shoulders she had heard the compliments that her mother received about her.

But she had known that while the men at any age looked at her with a certain glint in their eyes, the women on the other hand stiffened and looked down their noses, as if they thought her very appearance was somewhat reprehensible.

"I suppose I do look a little theatrical, Mama," she had said once.

Her mother had laughed.

"Nonsense! You are thinking about that ridiculous remark of your father's—that you could go on the stage because you dance well. Red hair is always supposed to be very theatrical, but actually, darling, you look very much a lady, and a very aristocratic one at that."

"Like my great-grandmother?"

"Exactly! We only have a miniature of her, but your father's father had a full-size portrait, although I do not know what happened to it."

"I never knew that before. Where is it?"

"At your grandfather's house, and when your father was away with the Regiment your grandfather died and the house was sold, and he never knew what happened to the contents."

"How disappointing!" Ilouka said. "I would love to have seen it."

"I expect it was very like the miniature we have, and the artist might in fact have been painting you."

The miniature, however, was rather faded, and although there was a distinct resemblance, Ilouka thought, she would have loved to see something of her great-grandmother which would have brought her more vividly to life than her imagination could do.

However it was only now, when she was eighteen, that Ilouka fully blossomed into what her mother knew was a beauty who would take the Social World by storm.

She had always been told how much the gentlemen of St. James appreciated a beautiful woman, and although she was her own child, she thought that it would be impossible to find anyone so lovely or so unusual as Ilouka.

Looking at her now in her travelling-clothes, which were simple enough but to which she gave a style and an elegance which could not be bought, she thought it was a terrible waste to send Ilouka off to dismal isolation in Bedfordshire.

She kissed her again and said:

"I will let you know the very moment you can come home. Take care of yourself, my precious one."

"I promise to do that, Mama."

Ilouka gave her a beguiling smile and went down the front-door steps to where her step-father's carriage was waiting.

Looking at the coachman on the box wearing his cockaded top-hat and the two horses with their silver harness, Lady Armstrong could not help wishing that her husband had been generous enough to send Ilouka all the way in it.

But they both had so much to thank him for that it would be stupid to resent his small meannesses.

There were not many of them, but as her first husband had said laughingly:

"Every man has a little of the miser and the spend-thrift in him. Unfortunately, as far as I am concerned, the balance is not very even and tips overwhelmingly towards the spend-thrift."

His wife had laughed.

"Darling, I have never known you to be miserly about anything," she had said.

"Only about the time I spend apart from you," the Colonel had replied. "Then I grudge every minute, every second we are not together."

He had kissed her and they forgot what they were talking about.

Now as the carriage carrying Ilouka drove away and Lady Armstrong waved until it was out of sight, she prayed:

"Please, God, let Ilouka find the love that her father gave to me and that I had with him."

It was a prayer that came from the very depths of her heart, and she knew that nothing she could wish for her daughter was more important than that she should find true love, which made everything else in the world vanish into insignificance.

Chapter Two

The Stage-Coach carrying Ilouka and Hannah was slow and uncomfortable.

It was a very old vehicle, as they had expected, because it was not on one of the main Highways where the quicker-moving, better-sprung one plied for hire.

But on the twisting country lanes there was no choice, and the Coach which went by once a day carried passengers from one village to another so that in most cases it stopped practically every mile.

Ilouka, who was always interested in people, talked to the fat farmers' wives who carried baskets of baby chicks, or to their young daughters who were travelling to nearby towns to go into service for the first time.

Hannah made it obvious that she disapproved of her conversing so familiarly, but Ilouka paid no attention to her or to the manner in which she sat stiff and unbending, replying in monosyllables to anybody who addressed her.

They stopped for luncheon at a country Inn with the inevitable village green in front of it and a duck-pond in which there were no ducks.

Fortunately, the Inn-Keeper was wise enough not to try fancy dishes for his customers, but produced home-cured ham and a local cheese which to Ilouka's mind was far more palatable than anything more pretentious but badly cooked.

She accepted a glass of home-made cider with her meal, although Hannah insisted on having tea because the water was boiled.

As Hannah was so disapproving and critical of everything, Ilouka could not help wishing that she was with somebody young with whom she could laugh, or, better still, her mother, who when they were alone invariably saw the funny side of everything.

She planned that when she was at Stone House with her step-father's sister, whom she had been told to call "Aunt Agatha," she would write to her mother every day, making it like a diary and trying to find things to tell her which would sound amusing.

'It is going to be difficult,' Ilouka thought with a wry smile, knowing that at Stone House the days followed one another with monotonous regularity, and usually nothing happened which was worth recalling.

They stopped at Market Town where the other occupants of the inside of the Coach alighted and two newcomers came to join Ilouka and Hannah.

They were certainly more interesting than any of the passengers who had been in the Coach before.

The man was elderly but had about him a certain raffish air which for the moment Ilouka could not recognize.

He was obviously not rich, although his clothes were smartly cut, and his overcoat, which he carried over his arm, had a velvet collar.

At first she thought it strange that he should be travelling by Coach. Then because she was observant she saw that his shoes, although highly polished, were worn and the white cuffs at his wrists were frayed at the edges.

After she had looked at the woman who accompanied him she decided that they were probably an actor and actress.

The woman was small and very attractive, with dark hair and flashing eyes made larger by the application of mascara on her eye-lashes.

Her lips were crimson, and Ilouka knew by the way Hannah's back became as stiff as a ramrod and she turned her face to look out the window that she disapproved.

As she and Hannah were sitting on the seat of the Coach which faced forward, the newcomers took possession of the seats opposite them, with their backs to the horses.

As the Coach began to move off again the actress, speaking for the first time, said:

"Well, thank the Lord we can rest our legs, and I personally am going to put mine up!"

As she spoke she seated herself sideways in her corner and put her legs up on her seat.

The man to whom she addressed her remark smiled.

"I think you're wise," he said. "You don't want to feel tired before you dance, although we'll have a night's rest before we get there tomorrow."

"In what sort of place?" the woman asked disparagingly.

"I hope it'll not be too uncomfortable," the man said apologetically, "but we'll certainly be in luxury tomorrow night."

The way he spoke with an unexpected lilt in his voice told Ilouka that he was looking forward to tomorrow and it meant something special to him.

She wondered where they were going and longed to ask them if they were in fact on the stage.

Then the man who was sitting opposite her looked at her for the first time, and she saw the expression of astonishment in his eyes.

It was something which often happened when men looked at her, and because it always made her shy she turned her face to look out the window at the passing countryside.

At the same time, she was well aware that the man was still staring at her, and they had not gone far before he said, and Ilouka was certain it was merely an excuse to speak to her:

"Excuse me, Madam, but would you allow me to open the window a little?"

His voice was deep, somehow melodious, and also surprisingly well educated.

"Yes, of course," Ilouka replied. "It has grown much hotter this afternoon and it will be nice to have some air."

"Thank you."

He started to let down the window with difficulty because the sash was old, the leather which held it in place was worn, and it was quite hard to fix it in place on the hooks provided.

Finally he achieved it, and when he had finished the actress said:

"I hope there's not going to be a draught. I don't want to have a sore throat by tomorrow morning."

"If it is too draughty for you," the elderly actor replied courteously, "I'll of course close it again."

"Oh, leave it for the moment!"

The man settled himself back in his seat facing Ilouka.

"I'm afraid this Coach is very slow," he said. "We've been waiting for it for over an hour."

"The horses are tired," Ilouka replied. "They have come a long way, poor things."

"I feel sorry for them too," the actor agreed, "but at least this Coach isn't over-laden, although I should have thought it was too heavy a vehicle for only two horses."

Hannah fidgeted ostentatiously and Ilouka knew she was annoyed that she should be talking to a stranger but was not quite certain how she could end the conversation.

Because she thought it tiresome that Hannah should be so unfriendly, she said:

"It always distresses me to see how Stage-Coaches wherever they are travelling usually carry far too many people and too much baggage for the horses which have to pull them. In fact, I have heard that the life of a horse drawing a Stage-Coach is little more than three years!"

"I agree with you, Madam, it's disgraceful!" replied the man to whom she was speaking. "And even though the service in most cases is lamentable, they still charge far too much for the fares."

"I told you we should have gone by Post-Chaise!" the young woman he was with said petulantly. "I can feel my bones rattling every time the wheels turn in this ramshackle old wheel-barrow!"

Ilouka laughed because the way she spoke was so funny, and it flashed through her mind that this would certainly be a conversation to relate to her mother.

As if she felt obliged to intervene, Hannah said:

"As we've still a long way to go, Miss Ilouka, I suggest you shut your eyes and rest. Otherwise, when we do get to the place we're staying you'll be too tired to sleep."

Ilouka smiled at her.

She was well aware that Hannah was trying to prevent her from talking to the man opposite, but she had no intention of being forced into silence until she had found out a little more about him.

"Will you tell me, Sir," she asked, "where you are going?"

"We're on our way, Miss Ganymede and I, to stay with the Earl of Lavenham!"

He spoke the name with a flourish as if he bowed while he did so.

"That's if we ever get there!" Miss Ganymede remarked. "And by the time we do I'll be rattled to bits, so it's very unlikely I'll be able to walk, let alone dance!"

"Are you a dancer?" Ilouka asked eagerly.

"I hope that's obvious," Miss Ganymede replied, "but you tell her, D'Arcy."

"Of course," the man answered. "Let me introduce myself, Madam—my name is D'Arcy Archer, at your service, and the lady beside me is Miss Lucille Ganymede from the Royal Olympic Theatre in London."

"How exciting!" Ilouka exclaimed. "I have heard of

the Royal Olympic Theatre. In fact I read in one of the newspapers that they were performing a Play called *Mary, Queen of Scots,* and I longed to see it."

"That's indeed correct, Madam," Mr. Archer replied. "You're very well informed."

"Was the Play successful?" Ilouka asked.

Mr. Archer gave what sounded a very theatrical laugh.

"One of the newspapers said last week that Wych Street, where the Olympic Theatre is situated, should henceforth be called 'Witch Street,' for great is the enchantment of Vestris and Foote."

As he spoke he looked up to see if she understood, and in case she did not, he explained:

"Madame Vestris, of whom you must have heard, Madam, is the owner of the Royal Olympic Theatre, and Miss Foote, a great actress, plays the part of Mary Stuart, Queen of Scots."

"I have heard of Madame Vestris," Ilouka replied.

As she said the name she remembered that her mother had in fact been shocked by the publicity which Madame Vestris had acquired by appearing on the stage in Plays in which she played the part of a man and showed her legs.

Thinking back, Ilouka could remember how the newspapers had been full of the part she played first in a Play called *Giovanni in London.*

Then she had worn breeches, and although Ilouka had been very young at the time, she could remember her mother saying it was quite outrageous and improper and she was only astonished that anybody would go to see such a Play.

Her father, however, had laughed.

"It is not the Play they go to see, my darling," he had said, "but Lucy Vestris's extremely shapely legs!"

"Really!" Mrs. Compton had exclaimed. "While I am certain the Theatre is full of men, no lady could be expected to watch such an immodest exhibition!"

Her father had laughed again, but because it had

intrigued Ilouka to think of a woman showing her legs, she had in the next few years read the notices that appeared about Madam Vestris in *The Beggar's Opera*, *The Duenna*, and *Artaxerxes*, where once again her legs were very much in prominence.

Because she knew it shocked her mother, she did not mention Madame Vestris to her, but some years later when she was with her father she asked:

"Have you seen this Madame Vestris, Papa, about whom the newspapers are always writing?"

"She is a very attractive woman," her father had answered, "but whether I was interested in her or not, she would be far too expensive for me."

He spoke without thinking, saw the puzzled expression on his daughter's face, and said quickly:

"Forget I said that. Your mother would not approve— what I was meaning was that the Bucks and Beaux of St. James's smother her with flowers, and the presents she receives are worth a very large sum of money."

After that Ilouka had watched the newspapers to learn more about Madame Vestris.

Three years ago she had seen sketches of her as "John of Paris" in skirts way above the knees, and as "Captain Macheath" dressed completely as a man in close-fitting pantaloons, a high cravat, and a top-hat on her head.

After her father's death, when her mother and she moved to Sir James's large and comfortable house, Ilouka had really forgotten Madame Vestris and the Theatres in London about which she had often talked to her father.

Now she found it absorbing to be actually speaking to an actor and an actress.

Because she was curious she asked:

"And do you also perform at the Royal Olympic Theatre, Mr. Archer?"

"Alas, I have not had that privilege," he replied, "but Miss Ganymede and I are on our way to give a private performance for the Earl of Lavenham and his friends, and I don't think His Lordship'll be disappointed."

As he spoke he looked towards Miss Ganymede and said:

"I know, Lucille, that His Lordship will appreciate the way you'll imitate Madame Vestris."

"I should jolly-well hope so," Miss Ganymede replied, "seeing the long way we've had to come to show what we can do!"

Ilouka noticed that while Mr. Archer's voice was cultivated, Miss Ganymede's had a common accent.

As if she wished to assert herself and prevent Mr. Archer from concentrating his attention on Ilouka, she said:

"I can feel a draught! For God's sake shut the window or I'll be hoarse tomorrow night and unable to sing a note!"

"Yes, of course, I'll close it at once," Mr. Archer said.

He bent forward and lifted the strap, but it was even more difficult to close the window than it had been to open it.

After a short struggle he put his top-hat down on the seat beside him and rose to his feet.

He gave the leather strap a mighty tug and it came away in his hand, with the result that instead of closing, the window slithered down and disappeared below the sill.

"Now see what you've done!" Miss Ganymede exclaimed.

"I'm sorry," Mr. Archer murmured, "but the strap is rotten, although I daresay I can raise the window without it."

He started to try to pull the glass up from where it had settled deep inside the door.

As he did so the Stage-Coach turned a corner and lurched so that Mr. Archer had to hold on to the window with both hands.

There was a shout from the coachman as he pulled in

his horses sharply and the Coach came suddenly to a halt.

It shook everybody inside so that Miss Ganymede gave a little scream, and Hannah, looking down her nose, said sharply:

"This is disgraceful! What's happening?"

The shouting outside went on although they could not hear what was said, but as the window was down Mr. Archer put his hand outside, opened the door, and stepped out into the road.

He stood staring ahead, then gave a sudden cry and came to the open door of the Caoch to say:

"Get out! Get out quickly!"

Because Ilouka was nearest to him he took her hand in his and pulled her forward out of the Coach.

Even as she reached the road, wondering what on earth was happening, the Coach in which they had been travelling seemed to sway for a moment, then fell sideways at a strange angle.

As it did so, the coachman threw down the reins and jumped from the box, and as Ilouka looked on in horror the whole Coach, with the horses plunging to save themselves, turned over, falling over the side of the road and a second later disappearing out of sight.

For a moment Ilouka could not believe that what had happened was not some figment of her imagination.

Yet the Coach had gone and she realised that she, Mr. Archer, and the coachman were standing on the road which ended abruptly about two feet away from them.

As she stepped forward to see what had happened, she could see the Coach lying upside-down about twelve feet below them amongst the debris of the road, on which there had apparently been a land-slide.

The horses were lying on their backs, their legs in the air, and neighing with fear, and she could see the Guard, who had been thrown clear in the fall, struggling to his feet and going towards the terrified animals.

Then as the coachman began to descend to where the

Coach was lying, Ilouka was aware that she was still
holding on tightly to Mr. Archer's hand.

"We must . . . help the . . . others," she gasped.

"Wait a minute," he replied. "I'm sure that even in
this isolated spot, help'll come from somewhere."

As he spoke he looked over his shoulder in the
direction from which they had come.

Sure enough, there were two men, obviously farm-
labourers, running towards them.

"How can . . . this have . . . happened?" Ilouka asked.
"Surely if the road had subsided they should
have . . . prevented us from . . . coming this . . . way?"

"It may only just have occurred," Mr. Archer replied.

Ilouka thought this was very likely, but for the moment she could think only of Hannah trapped in the
fallen vehicle and was at a loss as to what she could do
about it.

She went to the edge of the road, saying:

"I think, Mr. Archer, we should climb down."

But he held her back, saying:

"Be careful! I doubt if it'd be possible to release the
two women inside the Coach until there're enough men
to lift it."

The coachman and the Guard were struggling with
the horses, who were frightened to the point where it
was difficult to go near them.

Then, almost by magic, people began to arrive
seemingly from nowhere.

Afterwards Ilouka felt that they must have been
working in the fields, or perhaps the people in the
village they had just passed through instinctively became aware of the tragedy that had happened down the
road.

Anyway, there were men starting to try to raise the
Coach, men trying to release the horses, and others
who carried the trunks and other pieces of luggage
which had been stacked on the roof up onto the road.

"Now ye sit down, dearie, there's nought ye can do
by going down there," a motherly old woman said to

Ilouka when she tried to climb down the bank to where the Coach lay.

"I must see to my maid," she answered. "She is trapped inside!"

"Ye can't do no good," the woman replied. "Now sit ye down! It's hard, Oi know but women only gets in th' way at times like this."

Ilouka was obliged to admit that she was right, although she kept rising from the trunk on which she was seated to try to see what was happening.

She could see that the men were having great difficulty in moving the Coach, which seemed to have become embedded in two or three feet of mud.

It seemed to her that the methods by which they were working were uncoordinated, and while they kept shouting instructions to one another, nobody appeared to obey them.

Finally, after what seemed to Ilouka hours of anxiety when all she could think of was that Hannah must be suffering and was probably injured by the fall, the Vicar came to her side.

"I have been told that you are travelling with your maid, who is an elderly woman," he said.

"Is she all right?" Ilouka asked quickly.

"I am sorry to have to tell you that she is dead," the Vicar replied quietly. "And so is the other lady in the Coach."

* * *

Ilouka sat in the shabby Sitting-Room in the Vicarage with Mr. Archer.

She was trying to realise that she would never see poor Hannah again, never hear her sharp, disapproving comments, which more often than not had amused her because they were so characteristic of Hannah herself.

The Vicar's Housekeeper had given her and Mr.

Archer cups of strong tea and some sandwiches, which Ilouka had eaten mechanically without tasting them.

"I cannot believe it!" she said now.

"Nor can I," D'Arcy Archer replied quietly.

"I realise you saved... my life by pulling me out of the Coach," she said, "and I am very... grateful."

"It would have been better if I had died instead of that poor girl," Mr. Archer said. "I am an old man and I have lost my last chance, but there was no reason for her to die."

Because she thought it might be rude to seem unsympathetic, Ilouka asked:

"Why is it your last chance?"

"I don't suppose you would be interested," he said, "but I've been down in my luck of late."

"You mean you are not getting parts in the Theatre?"

"I think I have haunted the offices of every Theatrical Agent in London," D'Arcy Archer said bitterly, "but the only money I've been able to make was by singing and telling jokes in taverns, and the clientele of those places are not very generous."

"I am sorry," Ilouka said softly, as there seemed to be nothing else she could say.

"Then yesterday, out of the blue," D'Arcy Archer went on, "I had the chance of a lifetime."

"What was it?" Ilouka enquired.

"I was in an Agent's office, begging him almost on my knees to find me work. Even if it only brought in a few shillings I knew it would prevent me from starving."

He drew in his breath before he said:

"Yes, starving! The word may shock you, but it happens to be the truth."

"What happened?" Ilouka asked.

"He'd just told me that there was nothing and he was sick of seeing my ugly face," D'Arcy Archer answered, "when a letter was brought in to him by a groom in livery. The Agent, Solly Jacobs by name, took the note and opened it, and while he read it I waited.

"'You can tell your Master,' he said to the groom,

'that I've no-one who will go to the country when there's plenty of work for them here in London.'"

Ilouka was listening now, interested in what Mr. Archer was saying, and as if her attention encouraged him, he continued:

"Because I was desperate I said:

"'I'll go to the country!'

"Solly Jacobs laughed.

"'Oh, you would, would you? Well, His Lordship wants something pretty and new to entertain his friends.'

"'What does His Lordship want?' I asked quickly, in case the groom should leave.

"Solly Jacobs took the note and threw it across the desk at me.

"'See for yourself,' he said.

"I picked up the note, and I think my hands were trembling. I had a feeling that was almost clairvoyant that this would mean something to me, and perhaps my luck would turn."

"What did the letter say?" Ilouka asked.

"It said that the Earl of Lavenham required two high-class entertainers for a party he was giving at his house in Hertfordshire tomorrow night. He was prepared to pay any sum that was reasonable, provided he had the best."

D'Arcy Archer paused as if to see what impression his story had made on Ilouka. Then, because she did not speak, he said:

"You must have heard of the Earl of Lavenham, the best-known sportsman on any race-course, rich as Croesus, and beautiful women surround him like moths round a flame."

"No, I have never heard of him . . . at least I do not think so," Ilouka mused.

"Then you can take my word for it, he's the tops in the Social World," D'Arcy Archer said.

"Do go on with your story."

As he continued, D'Arcy Archer's air of despondency seemed to lift and he sounded quite animated.

"I said to Solly Jacobs:

"'If His Lordship wants the best, he can have it. You can leave that to me!'

"'What are you talking about?' Solly Jacobs enquired.

"'I'm telling you that I can supply the goods all right,' I replied.

"'And how can you do that?' he asked.

"'Well, I suppose you would think one of the leads from the *Olympic Revels* would please His Lordship and his friends?'

"'If you're talking about trying to get Madame Vestris,' Solly Jacobs said, 'you can forget it. She wouldn't demean herself to go out of London for any man, not even Lavenham!'

"'I wasn't thinking of Vestris herself' I replied, 'but what about her understudy?'"

D'Arcy Archer paused and laughed.

"You should have seen Solly Jacobs' face!

"'Are you certain you can get her?' he enquired.

"'Quite certain,' I replied. 'She's been playing a small part in the *Revels* and she also understudies Madame Vestris. At it happens, she's a relative of mine.'

"'I don't believe it!' Solly Jacobs said to me.

"'It's true!' I answered. 'Lucille Ganymede is her name, and she'll not come for peanuts! But I'll fix it up.'

"I knew as I spoke from the expression on Jacobs' face that he only half-believed me, but he had no wish to refuse to do what the Earl wanted. He sent the groom away, telling him to come back for an answer in two hours' time, then he said to me:

"'You've got two hours to fix it all up.'

"'I'll fix it,' I said, 'but now I want to know how much you are soaking His Lordship for.'

"'That's my business!' Jacobs said, 'But I'll make it worth your while, and the girl's. I'll give you fifty pounds all in. You pay the girl what she wants for her services, and I'll keep the rest.'"

D'Arcy Archer sighed.

"I knew 'the rest' would be a jolly heavy amount, but I was not disposed to argue. I knew that Lucille would not come cheap, but I also happened to know that she was hard up at the moment, had lost her Protector, and would at least listen to what I had to say."

"If she was acting at the Royal Olympic Theatre," Ilouka said, "how could she get away?"

"I can explain that," D'Arcy Archer said. "The last Season at the Royal Olympic has just ended. It started in January and finished in April, and Madame Vestris is having a rest, as is the rest of the cast, before they start up again."

"Oh, I understand!" Ilouka exclaimed. 'So Miss Ganymede was free!"

"Exactly!" D'Arcy Archer replied. "And she jumped at the opportunity of meeting the Earl. There's not an actress in London who hasn't tried to catch his eye when he sits in his Box at the Theatre."

D'Arcy Archer chuckled before he said:

"Going down on their knees most of them are, hoping he'll ask them out to supper, but he's known to be very fastidious, and as one of them said to me:

"'I'm more likely to be invited on a spree with the Man in the Moon than with the stuck-up Earl of Lavenham.'"

"Is he more important than any other gentleman?" Ilouka enquired.

"He is, and you would understand why if you saw him," D'Arcy Archer replied. "Top-lofty, an aristocrat to his finger-tips, and you're not likely to forget it."

He paused before he went on:

"And everything he touches turns to gold. His horses are nearly always first past the winning-post, gamblers go pale when they see him approaching the gaming-tables, and there is not a beautiful woman who doesn't fall into his arms like a ripe peach!"

Ilouka laughed because it sounded so funny.

"It is all very well to laugh," D'Arcy Archer said, and the despondent note was back in his voice, "but now you understand that without Miss Ganymede there is no point in my continuing my journey to the Earl's house."

His voice was bitter as he continued:

"I shall go back to London, tell Solly Jacobs I have failed, and you may be quite certain he'll want back what is left of his fifty pounds."

"It is not your fault," Ilouka said sympathetically.

"You tell that to Solly. He"ll have his 'pound of flesh,' and I am the one who'll have to give it to him!"

D'Arcy Archer suddenly threw himself back in his chair and put his hands over his eyes.

"What is the point of going on?" he asked. "I'm old, finished, and the sooner I'm in the grave, the better!"

He spoke dramatically, but Ilouka knew that he meant it.

She could understand how bitter it was for him to lose the chance of making some money.

Through the Earl's influence, if he was pleased, Mr. Archer might have got other engagements of the same sort, but he had now, in her father's words, been "pipped at the post."

'Poor man!' she thought.

She knew it was as hard for him losing the little actress as it was for her losing Hannah.

She knew how upset her mother would be that Hannah was dead, and although she could not pretend that she was a particularly lovable person, she had been part of her childhood, and she knew that in many ways she would feel lost without Hannah, especially when she was at Stone House.

At least Hannah would have been a buffer between herself and Mrs. Adolphus, but now she would be alone there, with nothing to do but control herself from answering back when her mother's name was disparaged and everything she did was somehow wrong.

She gave a deep sigh and thought that when the Vicar returned she would have to ask him how soon there would be another Coach to carry them on to the next part of the journey.

Almost as if to think of him conjured him up, the Vicar came into the Sitting-Room.

He saw down beside Ilouka and said quietly:

"I have arranged, Miss Compton, for your maid and the young lady to be buried tomorrow morning. Our local carpenter is making the coffins for them at this moment, and I thought if you wish to continue your journey there would be no point in waiting any longer."

"No . . . of course not," Ilouka replied, "and thank you very much for all the trouble you have taken."

She paused, then she asked:

"Is there anywhere in the village where I can stay the night?"

"You can stay here," the Vicar said quickly. "I thought I had already made that clear. I have told my House-keeper to prepare a room for you and another for Mr. Archer."

"That is very kind of you, Sir," D'Arcy Archer said.

"I am afraid you will find my house is not very luxurious," the Vicar said with a faint smile, "but at least the rooms are clean, which I rather doubt they would be at The Green Man."

"I am very grateful."

As Ilouka spoke she knew that her mother would be horrified at the idea of her staying alone without Hannah to chaperone and look after her at a public Inn, however small and unimportant it might be.

"At what time will there be a Stage-Coach tomorrow?" D'Arcy Archer said. "Not to take me in the same direction in which I was travelling today, but back to London?"

"That is something I shall have to find out," the Vicar replied. "I think there is a man in the kitchen at the moment who will be able to answer that question."

He rose and left the room, and when he had gone Ilouka said:

"I am so sorry for you, Mr. Archer. I wish I could help."

"I wish you could too," he replied.

Then, as if she had suddenly put the idea into his head, he looked at her and his eyes seemed to take in for the first time since the accident the beauty of her face, the grace of her slim body, and her tiny feet which peeped beneath her travelling-gown.

He sat up, bending towards her.

"Tell me, Miss Compton, can you sing?" he asked.

"I have always sung at home," Ilouka answered, "and actually, now that I think of it, one of the songs which my mother has played for me is one which was made famous by Madame Vestris. It is the Bavarian Girls' song called *Bring My Broom*."

D'Arcy Archer drew in his breath, and clasping his hands together so that he could control them, he said:

"And I am certain, almost certain, that you can dance."

Ilouka smiled at him and her eyes twinkled.

"Because that is something people often say to me," she answered, "I should now feel ashamed if I said 'no.' Actually, I love to dance!"

There was a little pause. Then D'Arcy Archer said in a voice which sounded strange:

"You know what I am asking you—no, not asking—begging, praying, pleading, beseeching you to do?"

Ilouka looked at him in surprise.

"What are you saying?"

"I am asking you save me—to give me the chance which I have just lost through fate, or perhaps by the intervention of the Devil!"

"I . . . I do not . . . understand."

"It is quite simple," D'Arcy Archer replied. "Would you, out of the charity of your heart, save a poor old man from starvation?"

"Are you asking me to . . . give you . . . money?" Ilouka enquired hesitatingly.

She felt it was rather embarrassing that Mr. Archer should plead with her in such a manner. But after what he had said she had in fact been wondering how, without offence, she could give him perhaps five pounds from the money she had with her for her travelling expenses.

"It is not a question of money," he said quickly in a low voice. "I want you to take Lucille's place. If you will do that, Miss Compton, you will literally and truly save my life!"

For a moment it seemed to Ilouka that she would not comprehend what he was asking her to do.

When he had enquired whether she could sing or dance she had thought he was just interested in acting, but it had never struck her for one moment that he was begging her to take an actress's place and go with him to fulfil an engagement he had with the Earl.

Now he had put it into words.

Her first instinct was to say it was something she could not possibly do. Then like a voice whispering insidiously in her ear she asked herself:

"Why not?"

It would undoubtedly be a kindness, and she was quite certain that the story Mr. Archer had told her was true and that his despair at losing Lucille was not assumed.

Then she thought how horrified and shocked her mother would be at such an idea.

At the same time, she could also see a picture of the bleak, ugly house waiting for her in Bedfordshire.

She could almost hear Mrs. Adolphus's scolding voice, and she knew she would feel that she was trapped in what was a particularly unpleasant prison for weeks, perhaps months, if Muriel could not wring a proposal out of Lord Denton quickly.

Now once again she realised how gloomy and lost she would be without Hannah.

At least the old maid was loyal to her mother and would in her own way somehow protect her from the worst unkindnesses that her step-father's sister would inflict upon her.

'If I do what Mr. Archer wants,' she thought, 'it will at least take one day off the time I have to spend at

Stone House; for even if Aunt Alice will have me, I
cannot stay there long because they are so poor, and I
might have to go back to Stone House.'

It all swept through her mind, not smoothly and
rhythmically like something that was pleasant, but jerk-
ily and disjointedly so that everything seemed worse.

'I cannot go there without Hannah,' Ilouka thought.

D'Arcy Archer was looking at her pleadingly, his
hands clasped together, his eyes somehow like a spaniel
dog's looking trustingly at its Master.

"I . . . I think . . . perhaps I rather exaggerated
my . . . talents," Ilouka said hesitatingly. "I am sure I am
not . . . good enough to do anything . . . professional that
you would . . . expect."

"I will be frank with you and say that while Lucille
danced quite well and could sing with quite a pretty
contralto voice—otherwise she would not have
understudied Madame Vestris—she had little personality, and she certainly was not in any way as beautiful as
you are."

He paused before he added impressively:

"I am not trying to flatter you, Miss Compton. I am
merely telling you the truth when I say that I think you
are the most beautiful girl I have ever seen in my whole
life!"

"Thank you," Ilouka said. "But while I want to help
you, Mr. Archer, you must realise that anything to do
with the theatrical profession, even though this particular entertainment takes place in a private house, would
seem very shocking to my mother."

"I think all mothers and Ladies of Quality treat the
stage with suspicion," D'Arcy Archer remarked, "but I
promise you, Miss Compton, I will look after you and
make quite certain that everybody treats you with
respect and propriety."

He paused before he continued:

"I happen to know that the Earl's interest is very
much engaged at the moment with a very talented
young actress who is appearing at Drury Lane, and in

the Social World he has the pick of all the Beauties who are toasted from one end of St. James's Street to the other!"

"What you are saying, Mr. Archer, is that in no circumstances is he likely to be interested in me," Ilouka said.

"I am trying to reassure you, Miss Compton, that your visit will not involve you with His Lordship, nor, I hope, any of his friends. In fact I have always been told that the Earl is very fastidious as to whom he entertains."

"You certainly seem to know a lot about him," Ilouka said.

D'Arcy Archer laughed.

"Perhaps I am presuming on knowledge which comes from hearsay—the chatter in the Theatre dressing-rooms and the gossip which occurs when men get together and discuss race-meetings and whose horses are most likely to win."

"I am sure I must have heard of the Earl in that connection," Ilouka said. "My father always followed the wins on the Turf, but I cannot remember the Earl winning either the Derby or the Gold Cup at Ascot."

"He did win the Derby three years ago," D'Arcy Archer contradicted, "but at that time his name was Hampton."

"Oh but of course!" Ilouka exclaimed. "Now I know whom you are talking about. He won with a horse called Apollo which my father said was the finest animal he had ever seen in his life."

"That is something I am sure the Earl would like you to tell him," D'Arcy Archer said.

Ilouka looked at him in a startled manner.

"I have not said that I will agree to your very strange and to me outrageous proposition."

"But you will, promise me you will? How can I tell you, Miss Compton, what it will mean to me? If you believe in answers to prayer, all I can tell you is that I'm praying fervently on my knees that you will not,

like the Pharisees, pass by on the other side, but be a
good Samaritan and save me."

Ilouka rose to her feet.

"You are making it very difficult for me to refuse you,
Mr. Archer, although I ought to do so."

"If we always did exactly what we ought to do, the
world would be a very dull place," D'Arcy Archer
replied. "Put this down to an adventure, Miss Compton,
something you will look back on and think that although
it was rather daring, it was at least an act of courage and
certainly one of most admirable Christian charity."

Ilouka walked to the window.

She looked out on the untidy, unkept garden, but she
did not see the shadows growing longer as the last
glimmer of the sun sank over the distant horizon.

Instead, she saw the flat fields of Bedfordshire stretching
away towards a grey horizon, and she could hear the
voice of Mrs. Adolphus, sharp as a needle, hurting her
with every word she said.

An adventure! Something exciting, something new,
something which would help a man who, through no
fault of his own, had lost the chance of a lifetime.

How could she refuse? How could she be so hard-
hearted as just to give him a few pounds and forget
him?

She turned from the window.

"I agree to what you have asked me to do, Mr.
Archer," she said quietly.

Chapter Three

Driving in a Post-Chaise, which D'Arcy Archer had found great difficulty in procuring, Ilouka thought it was certainly swifter and more comfortable than the Stage-Coach.

They had missed the latter because it passed through the village earlier in the day, when they were attending the Funerals of Hannah and Lucille Ganymede.

As they stood at the open graves in the small Church-yard where most of the tomb-stones were hundreds of years old, Ilouka felt that what was happening could not in fact be reality.

It seemed impossible that she had left home with Hannah, being her usual oppressive, rather disagree-able self, and now, by the mere chance of where she had sat in the Coach, she was dead.

'If I had been sitting where she was,' Ilouka thought, 'I, like the young actress, would have died, and Hannah would still be alive.'

But one could only attribute what had happened to fate or to the direction of some Power which was beyond the comprehension of man and for which there was no intelligible explanation.

Whatever the reason for Hannah's death, Ilouka tried to pray fervently for her soul and that she would find peace and happiness in Heaven.

She was aware that Mr. Archer, standing beside her, was looking sad and very old.

It was as if with the death of the young actress he had brought from London he had lost not only his hopes and ambitions for the future but perhaps the last remnant of his youth.

Then Ilouka told herself that she was being imaginative, and what she must do was follow the Burial Service word by word and pray for the souls of those who had left this world.

When she had thanked the Vicar for his kindness and hospitality and had given his Housekeeper such a large tip for her services that she could hardly believe her eyes, Ilouka was glad to be able to leave.

She knew it was an episode in her life that she would want to forget, especially the terrifying moment when she had watched the Stage-Coach overturn and disappear down the small cliff where the road had collapsed.

She had learnt from the Vicar that one horse had broken its leg and had to be destroyed, and the other was very shaken by the accident and would have to rest for several days.

'That is one good piece of news, at any rate,' Ilouka thought.

She was quite certain that those who ran the Stage-Coach would hurry it back onto the road as quickly as possible.

D'Arcy Archer told her when he came down to breakfast that he had sent to the nearest Inn which could provide a Post-Chaise.

"It will take a little time to get here," he said, "but I could not ask you to travel in a Stage-Coach again, even if we had been able to catch the one that passed through here at eight o'clock this morning."

"I must admit it would make me nervous," Ilouka replied.

"What is more," D'Arcy Archer went on in a somewhat embarrassed tone, "I thought, Miss Compton, that as you are not a poor actress living on her earnings, you would not perhaps—require as large a—remuneration for your—services as Lucille demanded."

For the moment Ilouka found it difficult to reply. Then she said:

"I hope you will understand, Mr. Archer, that I am doing this entirely to help you, and I would not in any circumstances accept payment for what in your own words is an 'act of charity.'"

She saw by the smile which came to Mr. Archer's lips and the expression in his eyes that this was what he had hoped she would say and was delighted that he could keep all the money for himself.

"I can only hope," Ilouka went on, "that I am successful tonight, and that His Lordship and perhaps his friends will engage you for other parties, for which you can replace Miss Ganymede with an equally accomplished actress."

"One day, perhaps," D'Arcy Archer replied in a low voice, "I shall be able to thank you for your kindness, but at the moment I find it difficult to express myself in words."

"Then please say nothing," Ilouka begged.

As soon as they set off in the Post-Chaise, the professional in D'Arcy Archer came to the surface and he began to explain to Ilouka exactly what he expected from her that evening.

"Usually on these occasions" he said, "the actors perform in the Dining-Room while the gentlemen are drinking their port and still sitting at the table."

Ilouka looked surprised.

"I suppose I somehow expected that anybody as rich as the Earl of Lavenham would have a private Theatre, or certainly a Music-Room where such performances would take place."

"I'm sure that His Lordship possesses both," D'Arcy Archer answered, "but this'll be far more informal and in fact a very *de luxe* and aristocratic version of the drinking-taverns where I've given my performances of late."

He spoke as if it had not been a very pleasurable experience, and Ilouka quickly changed the subject by asking him what the programme would be.

"First I'll play some spirited music . . . " he began.

"You are a pianist, Mr. Archer?" Ilouka interrupted.

"I started that way in an Orchestra at the Italian Opera House," he said, "but I soon wished to express myself as a person rather than as one of a team, so I struck out on my own."

"What did you do?"

"You name it, and I've done it!" D'Arcy Archer said. "I've taken parts in Plays by Shakespeare, I've travelled about the country, I've sung, danced, and at one time or another accompanied some very fine singers."

"It must have been very interesting," Ilouka said.

"Yes, but now I'm old," he remarked, "and nobody wants old men."

He spoke so sadly that Ilouka once again felt very sorry for him.

Then, as if he had no wish to depress her, he continued with his instructions on what they would do.

"I'll get them laughing," he said, "with jokes and songs at the piano which it'd be best for you not to listen to."

Ilouka looked surprised, and he explained:

"This is a party of gentlemen, Miss Compton, and I don't think there'll be any ladies present."

Ilouka felt as if he was a little doubtful on this score.

She did not realise that D'Arcy Archer was using "ladies" as the operative word and that the Earl might easily be entertaining a very different class of women, which would undoubtedly shock anyone as young as Ilouka.

Then he told himself that he was being needlessly apprehensive.

"Where we're going," he said aloud, "is the Earl's country seat, the home of the Hampton family, who are distinguished the length and breadth of England."

As he spoke he was quite certain that whatever the

Earl might do in London, he would not bring women of doubtful virtue into his home.

Because he was silent, Ilouka prompted:

"And when you have finished singing, what happens then?"

"I announce you as somebody very talented and very original, and you'll come on and sing a song."

"What song?"

"That we'll have to sort out at rehearsal, which, incidentally, we should have as soon as we arrive."

D'Arcy Archer paused before he said:

"You told me that you know *Bring My Broom*, which Madame Vestris sings so brilliantly, but I'm not certain it's really suitable for you. Tell me what other popular songs you know."

"I was thinking about that last night," Ilouka replied. "I know *The Mountain Maid*, *The Month of Maying*, and a ballad from *The Beggar's Opera*."

"Then we have a good choice," D'Arcy Archer said with a smile, "and we'll choose one which'll show you to your very best advantage."

"Thank you," Ilouka said.

"After that, you dance," he went on. "Now, what sort of music do you want for that? Without even having seen you perform, Miss Compton, I'm sure, that you're a very light and graceful dancer."

"I hope so," Ilouka replied, "but you are well aware that I am not in the least professional."

"That is immaterial."

"Then if I have a choice, and you happen to know any," Ilouka said, "I would like to dance to gypsy music. I have Hungarian blood in my veins, and the mere sound of one of their melodies, which should really of course be played on the violin, makes me want to dance, and my feet feel as if they have wings."

She knew that Mr. Archer was pleased by what she had said.

As they drove on he hummed various pieces which seemed to her very melodious and which she was sure would inspire her to dance in the way she had danced for her father, which had always pleased him.

On the way they stopped for a glass of cider at a Posting-Inn where they also changed horses. Then they set off again at a good pace.

"At this rate we should arrive at four o'clock this afternoon," D'Arcy Archer said. "I hope, Miss Compton, you'll not be too tired for us to run over your song and also choose the music you desire for your dance?"

"I am not tired," Ilouka replied, "although I did stay awake rather a long time last night, thinking of poor Hannah."

"Try to forget it," D'Arcy Archer advised. "It was a terrible experience which I'm sure could only happen once in a lifetime and will never occur again."

"I hope not," Ilouka replied.

As they drove on she was in fact feeling guilty, not so much about Hannah but because she was going about with a stranger to stay in a private house to which she had not been invited personally.

However, she considered that the alternative of rumbling along in a Stage-Coach alone to Aunt Agatha's house in Bedfordshire was a far worse proposition.

"At least when I do get there," she told herself, "I shall have something to think about and remember, which will make the misery of that dismal house seem not so oppressive."

At the same time, she was well aware that she was behaving in a most reprehensible manner and that it would give Mrs. Adolphus a heart-attack if she ever learnt about it.

"Only Papa would understand that I have no wish to turn my back on an adventure," Ilouka told herself.

However, she was well aware that she was just making excuses for something she wished to do.

When she glanced at Mr. Archer she realised that he was indeed a very old man, and if he was not smiling and making himself agreeable, his face in repose looked almost like a mask.

The lines at the sides of his eyes and from his nose to his mouth were so prominent that she could understand why he found it so difficult now to obtain a part on the stage.

"At least with the money he will earn from this he will be comfortable for a short while," she told her conscience.

She thought that if she had refused him it would be something for which she would undoubtedly reproach herself for the rest of her life.

Then, when a little earlier than D'Arcy Archer had expected the Post-Chaise turned in through a huge stone gateway surmounted by a coronet, Ilouka felt excited.

There was a long avenue of ancient oaks and at the end of it a magnificent house which she recognised as early Georgian with a lofty central block and two wings stretching out from it, making the whole a picture that was architecturally superb and of great beauty.

She was aware that Mr. Archer was impressed, but neither of them spoke as the Post-Chaise crossed a bridge at the narrow end of a large lake on which black and white swans moved serenely over the silver water.

They drew up outside a long flight of stone steps which led to the front door.

As they did so, footmen in green and yellow livery, which Ilouka recognised as the Earl's racing-colours, came hurrying down the steps to help them from the Post-Chaise and lift down the luggage from the back of it.

D'Arcy Archer paid their driver, then walked up the steps in a manner which told Ilouka he was acting the role of a lofty, authoritative Gentleman of Fashion.

The Butler greeted them, but not exactly with the kind of respect, Ilouka thought, that he would have done if she were arriving as herself.

"I think, Sir," he said to D'Arcy Archer, "you're the entertainers His Lordship told me to expect. Your bedrooms are ready for you, and on His Lordship's instructions there's a Sitting-Room adjoining them where there's a piano which His Lordship felt you might require."

"That is extremely considerate," D'Arcy Archer replied. "And is His Lordship at home at the moment?"

"No, Sir," the Butler replied. "His Lordship and his guests are at the races."

They were shown upstairs by a footman and taken along a corridor at the far end of which was a Suite consisting of two bedrooms with a Sitting-Room between them in which there was an upright piano.

Because it looked slightly out-of-place, Ilouka was sure it had been added as a concession to their profession.

She thought, as Mr. Archer had said, that it was considerate of the Earl to think it might be needed.

Then she remembered what Mr. Archer had told her about his being attached to a very talented actress who was appearing at Drury Lane, and thought he must have learnt from her what entertainers required.

Their luggage was brought upstairs and two housemaids appeared to unpack for Ilouka.

Because she had brought a great number of things with her for her stay in Bedfordshire, thinking perhaps it would mitigate her depression if she had the satisfaction of knowing she looked nice, she instructed them to unpack only the things she would need for the night.

Then she was puzzled for the moment by seeing that there were not only her own two trunks in the room but also another very shabby one which she did not recognise.

She was about to ask for it to be removed to Mr. Archer's room when she realised that it must have belonged to Lucille Ganymede.

Then she suddenly thought that if the actress had understudied Madame Vestris and sung the songs she had made so famous, she would undoubtedly dress in men's clothing.

It flashed through Ilouka's mind that Mr. Archer might expect her to do the same thing.

Then she told herself she was being needlessly apprehensive.

However, Lucille Ganymede's trunk in her room made her feel uneasy, first because it belonged to a woman who was dead, and secondly because it contained clothes which she considered immodest and indecent.

She pointed it out to one of the housemaids, saying:

"This trunk contains 'props' which, as it happens, I shall not need for our act this evening. Will you remove it from here and place it either in the Sitting-Room or somewhere outside until we leave?"

"Very good, Miss," the housemaid replied.

As they unpacked, Ilouka realised they were looking at her with curious eyes, almost as if she were an unknown species of female.

It amused her, and when she changed her travelling-gown for one of the simple but expensive dresses which her mother had bought for her in London, she went into the Sitting-Room to find Mr. Archer already seated at the piano.

He went on playing and said without turning round: "Is this the sort of music you like?"

He ran his fingers over the keyboard and began to play a melody which immediately conjured up pictures in Ilouka's mind of the gypsy musicians with their colourful clothes and painted caravans.

She listened with delight until D'Arcy Archer turned his head to say:

"I'm waiting to hear your verdict, Miss Compton."

"It is perfect!" Ilouka replied. "But if you will forgive me, I do not wish to practise my dance. I prefer to react spontaneously to the music when I hear it."

"There speaks the true professional!" he exclaimed. "At the same time, if I'm to accompany you for your songs, I think we should practise them."

"Yes, of course," Ilouka agreed.

However, they were interrupted when two footmen brought in a tray of delicious paper-thin sandwiches and a large selection of cakes which made Ilouka, after her simple luncheon, feel quite greedy.

She noticed that Mr. Archer ate hungrily, as if he was afraid the food would disappear before he had time to enjoy it.

Later thinking it over, she was certain he had at times been near to starvation and was afraid it would happen to him again.

'If I have a chance,' she thought, 'I will ask the Earl to recommend him to his friends. If that happens, at least for a time he will not starve and will not be so afraid for the future.'

After tea they tried out two or three songs, then D'Arcy Archer said he preferred her singing of *The Mountain Maid* and insisted that she go to have a rest.

"I want you to be very good tonight," he said, "and look like Persephone herself coming down into the darkness of Hades."

Ilouka laughed.

"That would hardly be polite to our host, and anything less like Hades than this lovely and impressive house I could not imagine."

She spoke lightly, and she did not see the expression of apprehension in D'Arcy Archer's eyes, almost as if he was afraid for her in a way he had no wish to express.

* * *

Ilouka was in bed and almost asleep when she heard in the Sitting-Room an authoritative voice speaking to Mr. Archer.

At first it was just a sound that seemed to mingle with her thoughts, which had almost become dreams.

Then it became real and she was aware of it and was sure that their host had returned and was doubtless giving Mr. Archer his instructions for the evening.

As she listened to it she thought the voice was exactly what she had expected from what she had heard about the Earl of Lavenham—clear and authoritative, and yet cold, distant, and undoubtedly condescending as he spoke to an inferior.

'I suppose,' she thought, 'that with all his possessions and the adoration he receives as a sportsman, and with all those beautiful women running after him, he is abominably conceited.'

She did not know why, but she felt at that moment almost hostile towards the Earl, although she had never seen him.

It was as if she were really a poor, aspiring actress hoping by his patronage to further her career and, like Mr. Archer, praying that the Earl's approval would somehow change her whole future.

After her father's death Ilouka had known what it was like to be very poor and be frightened of being entirely without money, so she had a kindred feeling for anybody in the same position.

She could hear Mr. Archer's voice, and although she could not hear what he said, she was aware that he was being humble and ingratiating.

It was almost as if he went down on his knees in front of the Earl.

'It is wrong,' she thought, 'that one man should have so much and others so little, and I doubt if he has any sympathy for the under-dog.'

She told herself again that she would do everything in her power to make the Earl help Mr. Archer, and wondered if it would be possible to speak to him alone while she was staying here.

But she expected that when they had finished their act they would merely leave the Dining-Room, or wherever they were performing, and in the morning be sent away like unwanted baggage and never thought of again.

Then there was silence in the next room and she knew the Earl had left.

'He has given his orders,' she thought, 'and all we have to do is to obey them to the letter!'

Because she was so tired she fell asleep.

* * *

Waiting behind the curtains which separated the main Dining-Room from the dais on which they were to perform, Ilouka could hear the voices and laughter of the guests the Earl was entertaining.

She was also vividly aware how nervous Mr. Archer was, and she thought with a smile of amusement that he might be the amateur and she the professional.

She was not worried for herself because she knew that if the Earl's guests did not appreciate her it would not matter at all to her, and only Mr. Archer would suffer.

She wanted to give a good performance for his sake, and because she had already conceived what was almost a dislike of their host, she longed to make him realise that he was not omnipotent.

At the same time, she was being needlessly critical when it would have been impossible to find fault with the way in which they had been treated so far.

Although Ilouka was aware that the rooms which they had been given were certainly not the best in the house, they were nevertheless very comfortable, and the piano had been provided especially for them.

The meal which had been served in their Sitting-Room, at the same time as the Earl and his guests dined downstairs, was excellent, and there was a bottle of wine which D'Arcy enjoyed, although Ilouka preferred lemonade.

All the time she knew that within herself there was a growing resentment at finding herself in an inferior position, which was something she had never known before in her life.

Mockingly she told herself it was a salutary experience which she would never forget.

However, there was nothing she could put her hand on positively that brought it home to her so vividly.

It was just the Earl's tone of voice when he was speaking to Mr. Archer and the way they were served the dinner, which although correct made Ilouka feel that the footmen, like the housemaids, were regarding them with curiosity rather than respect.

Then there was the house itself.

As they walked through it on their way to the Dining-Room, Ilouka had a glimpse of a huge Salon lit with crystal chandeliers and saw a unique collection of paintings and fabulous furniture.

As she peeped surreptitiously through the curtains into the Dining-Room itself, she told herself again that the Earl possessed too much.

She was looking at his possessions when she saw him.

He was sitting at the end of a long table which in the fashion set by George IV was polished and without a table-cloth, and on it were ornaments of both silver and gold which were breathtaking.

After a quick glance at them, Ilouka found herself looking at the man who sat at the far end in a high-backed armchair and knew that the Earl was actually exactly as she had expected him to be.

His friends whom he was entertaining, and there were about twenty or more, all men, were laughing uproariously and appeared to be enjoying themselves with an exuberance which she thought must have come after a good day's racing.

But she thought that the Earl in contrast looked supercilious and almost bored.

He was better-looking then she had expected, with straight classical features, hair swept back from a high forehead, and even at a distance she thought that in his evening-clothes with a high cravat round his long neck he was magnificent.

At the same time, he gave the impression of sitting aloof on a pinnacle of his own making, and with no intention of stepping down from it to mix with the common herd.

'He is too proud and too puffed up with his own importance,' she thought.

She pulled the curtain to, in case he should be aware that there was someone peeping at him.

The small stage or dais on which they were to perform stood between two pillars in the Dining-Room.

Ilouka thought it was probably used on other occasions by a Band or perhaps quite frequently for entertainment such as they were to give tonight.

The piano, D'Arcy Archer found with satisfaction, was an excellent one, and there were several lamps on the edge of the dais to act as footlights.

After some consideration as to what she should wear, Ilouka had chosen what she thought was one of her prettier gowns, which her mother had bought for her to wear at smart parties or a Ball.

It was not white, which would have been conventional for a débutante, but very pale green, with a full skirt which billowed out from a tiny waist and with puffed sleeves of the same material.

The décolletage displayed Ilouka's white skin, which her father had said had a magnolia-like quality about it.

The only ornamentation she wore was round her neck: a little cameo set with tiny diamonds that was hung on a ribbon of the same colour as her gown.

She had taken a great deal of trouble in arranging her hair in a much more elaborate manner than her mother felt was correct for a young girl.

Because she had long hair and the colour of it shone in the light, she arranged it in curls at the back of her head so as to make her look, in her own eyes at any rate, very theatrical.

It certainly framed her small heart-shaped face, and because despite her resolution to remain very calm she was excited, her eyes seemed enormous.

They had little glints of gold in the green of them, which made anyone who looked at her find it hard to look away.

As a concession to her theatrical appearance she had tied ribbons of the same colour round her wrists and added to each one a small white rose which actually belonged to another gown.

At the last moment she placed two of the same roses on top of her head and knew that they gave her the spring-like look of Persephone that Mr. Archer had envisaged.

When she had gone into the Sitting-Room where he was waiting for her, he stared at her for a long moment before he said:

"You look exactly as I hoped you would, and there is nothing more I can add to that."

"Thank you," Ilouka replied. "I am only afraid that I may let you down."

"I think that is impossible," he said. "We shall know by the end of the evening whether we are a success or a failure, but I am quite certain that the latter is a word which we need not include in our vocabulary."

Ilouka smiled.

"Papa always said that if you want to win the race you must believe yourself the winner."

"And that is what we must do," D'Arcy Archer said. "Now come, it is time we went downstairs, but before we do so, let me thank you once again for coming to my rescue."

As he spoke he took her hand in his and kissed it with a theatrical gesture which made Ilouka want to laugh.

Instead she accepted his tribute gracefully and they walked down the Grand Staircase side-by-side, while the footmen in the Hall watched them appreciatively.

When they were shown into the back of the Dining-Room and heard the noise made by the diners, Ilouka wondered how it would be possible for them to hold the attention of the Earl and his friends.

She thought it would be extremely humiliating to their self-esteem if they were either ignored or hissed off the stage.

Then she knew that even if they were not interested

in her personally it did not matter, and only Mr. Archer would suffer.

'I will do my best for his sake,' she thought. 'Then it is in the lap of the gods.'

She knew the dinner was coming to an end when the port had been taken round the table and decanters and others filled with brandy was set in front of the Earl.

He raised his voice and Ilouka heard him say:

"Now, Gentlemen, there will be a short entertainment to amuse you, and tonight it will be something that has not appeared here before."

"You are making me curious, Vincent," one of the Earl's guests remarked.

"Then I will reveal my surprise," the Earl said. "I am sure all of you know Madame Vestris!"

There was a murmur of assent and approval before the Earl went on:

"Madame unfortunately could not join us this evening, but we have in her place her understudy, and one who I am told is as attractive and as redoubtable as Lucy herself and—dare I say it?—somewhat younger in years!"

There was laughter at this and the Earl went on:

"Madame has captured the hearts of far more of us than I wish to disclose. Let us hope that her understudy will prove to be another Lucy as she was when she first captivated, entranced, and undoubtedly scandalised the *Beau Monde* eleven years ago."

There was more laughter and one or two men clapped their hands.

Then as if this was his signal to begin, D'Arcy Archer started to play the lilting, gay tune he had described to Ilouka.

Hidden behind the curtains, she heard the hush from the Dining-Room as the music started.

Then as Mr. Archer burst into song she realised that he had a deep baritone voice, which had however deteriorated with age, although his enunciation made it easy to hear every word he said.

She realised from the laughter that he evoked with almost every line that the song was appreciated by those listening to it.

At the same time, she found it hard to understand.

She told herself there must be a *double entendre* of some sort because a quite simple phrase had those listening laughing uproariously.

After a number or two she ceased to listen, and moving back to her peephole in the curtains she looked through it to discover the Earl's reaction.

As she had somehow expected, he was not laughing. Instead she thought there was a faintly contemptuous smile on his face, which annoyed her.

As he leant back in his chair, very much at his ease with a glass of what she thought must be brandy in his hand, she had the idea that while his friends had all eaten and drunk well, he had been abstemious.

She might have been wrong, but while their faces were flushed and in some cases riotously red, the Earl looked cool and athletic, and the jokes, if that was what they were in the song, did not make him laugh.

'Perhaps he will recommend Mr. Archer even though he personally is not very impressed with him,' Ilouka thought.

She had a feeling he was far from impressed and told herself that if Mr. Archer could not please the Earl she must certainly do so.

When the song came to an end, D'Arcy Archer told two or three jokes, which again Ilouka did not understand, and now she realised that at any moment it would be her turn.

She had an uncomfortable feeling that everything depended on her being a success.

The laughter died away as D'Arcy Archer said:

"And now, M'Lords and Gentlemen, I have the privilege of introducing a Lady who, when you see her, you will agree is like a nymph rising from the lake below the house, or perhaps a sprite who has crept in from the woods which surround us, or more likely, just a goddess who has stepped down from Olympus because she wishes to bemuse and bewitch the human race.

"Yes, that is right! It is a goddess I have here, and therefore, Gentlemen, let me present to you the Goddess Ilouka, here in person, for one performance and one only, before she returns to the place from whence she came."

It was all very dramatic, and it took Ilouka by surprise that he should call her by her own name.

At the same time, she was glad that she was not in fact having to impersonate somebody who was dead.

Then as D'Arcy Archer returned to the piano and played the first chords of *The Mountain Maid* she came slowly and gracefully onto the dais to stand in the centre of it.

Just for a moment she felt as if her voice had gone, then as if she was drawn to him like a magnet she looked towards the Earl.

As the words of the ballad rang out in her very musical voice, which, although she had no idea of it, had an almost hypnotic quality about it, she sang to him and him alone.

She saw that he was watching her, and while he leant back in his chair, apparently uninterested, she was almost certain that she held him with the vibrations of life flowing towards him from within herself with a magnetism which she forced him to acknowledge.

When the ballad had finished she made a little curtsey and the applause from the Earl's guests was unanimous and noisy.

The Earl did not clap, but his eyes were still on her face and Ilouka had the idea that although he would not show it, he had thought her good.

D'Arcy Archer was already playing the gypsy music they had chosen to which she would dance, and she stood very still, drawing in her breath, trying now to think not of the Earl but of the music itself so that it should inspire her.

Almost like a picture in front of her eyes she could

see the Hungarian Steppes as she envisaged them, the mountains in the distance topped with snow, and a band of gypsies camped round an open fire, their piebald horses cropping the grass, the women sitting in the doorways of the painted caravans.

The men placed their violins under their chins and the dancers came running towards them to dance to the music which ran in their blood.

It was then as she saw it all happening that Ilouka became one with the dancers, and her feet began to move.

Because D'Arcy Archer was a professional he knew instinctively what she wanted. At first the music was slow and soft and spoke of the gypsy's yearning which came from his soul as he searched for love, which was part of his heart.

Sometimes he found it, but sometimes he must move on to search for it in other lands, an El Dorado which was always beyond the farthest horizon, then beyond again.

Ilouka moved and swayed and translated into rhythm the music which flowed from Mr. Archer's fingers.

There was complete and absolute silence as her whole being stirred towards the adventure of life, not only of the spirit and the soul but also of the body.

The music quickened and Ilouka's feet seemed to fly over the polished floor until to those watching her it was as if she flew in the air above it.

She moved quicker and quicker, her arms in graceful harmony with her feet, her head thrown back, her eyes brilliant with a strange ecstasy which was part of the music, part of the feelings rising within herself.

Then those who were watching began to move their feet and hands in rhythm like the slow thump of drums.

They moved quicker and quicker until finally, as if she had attained what she sought and desired, she stood for a moment absolutely still.

Her arms were flung up towards the ceiling and her head was thrown back in rapture before finally she sank down to the floor, an indescribable gesture of surrender to forces greater than herself.

At a signal from D'Arcy Archer, with the final crescendo of music, the footmen closed the curtains.

The applause in the Dining-Room was deafening and several of the guests rose to their feet, shouting: "Bravo!" while others cried: "Encore!"

D'Arcy Archer rose from the piano to take Ilouka's hand and raise her to her feet.

He realised, as only a professional could, that for a moment it was difficult for her to come back to reality from the magic world into which her dancing had taken her.

"You were magnificent!" he exclaimed.

She gave him a faint smile before the curtains were pulled open, and the pressure of his hand told her that she must curtsey as he bowed to the applause in the Dining-Room.

Then as the curtains were shut again, there was a cry of: "Join us, join us. We went to talk to you!"

The footmen in charge of the curtains hesitated a moment, but Ilouka, as if suddenly aware of the men applauding her, remembered that she was the only woman in the room and said quickly:

"No! No!"

She did not wait for Mr. Archer to accompany her, but before he would say anything, taking her hand from his she fled through the door by which they had entered the Dining-Room and ran along the corridor and up the stairs.

She could not put it into words, but she knew that what she was encountering, although she had not expected it, was another dangerous situation.

Chapter Four

Upstairs in her bedroom, Ilouka sat down on the
stool in front of the dressing-table and waited for the
tremulous beating of her heart to subside and her
breath to come more easily from between her lips.

She felt as if she had been through a deep emotional
experience and it was hard to face normality and herself
again.

She knew that she had never before danced so well
or put so much feeling into her movements.

She was aware that first it was because she was trying
her best to help Mr. Archer since for his sake so much
depended on her, but also because she had been carried away by having an audience and especially the
Earl.

It had not been her main object to impress him, but
because she wanted to help Mr. Archer she had somehow stepped into the part so that she became temporar-
ily the Hungarian dancer she imagined herself to be
and was no longer Ilouka Compton.

Now she had to make the transition back to what she
thought of as her ordinary, prosaic self, and journey to
Bedfordshire to stay with an extremely disagreeable old
woman because her step-sister was jealous of her.

And yet for the moment that was the fantasy and
what she had been feeling inside herself was real.

Slowly her heart-beat returned to its normal pace and she looked at herself in the mirror opposite her.

Although her eyes were still shining brilliantly, she felt that her face now looked familiar and she had in fact become Ilouka again.

Then there was a knock on the door, and thinking it was one of the housemaids she called out:

"Come in!"

To her surprise, when the door opened it was a footman who stood there.

"His Lordship's compliments, Miss, and he'd be obliged if you'd join him in the Salon."

This was something which Ilouka had somehow not expected, and her first instinct was to refuse.

After all, she had played her part, she had entertained His Lordship's guests, and she thought it was unreasonable of him to demand more.

Then as the words of refusal sprang to her lips, she thought that if she did not do what he asked, perhaps it might harm Mr. Archer.

She was quite certain in her own mind that the applause she had received from the Earl's guests would have impressed him.

If that was so, he would probably ask Mr. Archer to entertain his guests at other parties he gave and also might recommend him to his friends.

However, she remembered that the Earl had not applauded her as his friends had done, and if she refused to obey his request, he might in his authoritative way make Mr. Archer suffer for her omission.

'It is the sort of thing he would do,' Ilouka thought, 'because he thinks everybody must obey him, and he ignores our personal thoughts and feelings because we are of no consequence.'

It made her angry to think such things, and yet they were inescapable.

If she were her own master, she thought, she would send a message to the Earl saying that she had fulfilled her part of the contract for which he had paid, was tired, and had no wish to do anything else except retire to bed.

Then she thought that if she sent such a reply it was doubtful if the footman would be brave enough to repeat it.

She felt herself smile at the thought of how angry the Earl would be simply because he was being defied by an actress of no importance whom he expected to be obsequiously grateful for his even noticing her.

'Whatever my own feelings, I must help Mr. Archer,' she decided.

She knew that the footman was looking at her curiously, as if he could not understand her hesitation, and after a deliberate pause she said:

"Please inform His Lordship that I will join him in a few minutes."

"Very good, Miss," the footman replied, then with a grin he added impudently: "You'd better make 'em short. His Lordship don't like waiting."

He shut the door as he spoke and did not hear Ilouka laugh.

Then because she refused to be hurried she deliberately tidied her hair and smoothed down her gown, and after quite a long look at her reflection in the mirror she walked slowly along the passage which led to the Grand Staircase.

As she went she could not help thinking how horrified her mother would be if she knew what she was doing.

It was also a pity that Muriel was not in her place to enjoy the experience of meeting a large number of gentlemen without any competition.

The thought of Muriel made her begin to hope fervently that Lord Denton, who was now staying at The Towers, would become so enamoured of her that he would propose marriage.

'If they get married quickly, I can go back home to Mama,' she thought, and knew that was what she wanted more than anything else.

As she reached the Hall a footman went eagerly ahead of her to open the door to the Salon.

As she reached it there was the noise of voices and loud laughter. But although it sounded very gay, Ilouka thought it was not the sort of party that would be considered correct for a débutante.

"But that is what I am not allowed to be," she excused herself.

At the same time, as the footman flung open the door she had to force herself to lift her chin and walk forward slowly and with a composure that she was not feeling.

There was quite a distinct hush as she moved down the big room beneath the lighted chandeliers, and although she felt shy and tried to focus her eyes, she could see nothing but a blur of faces.

Then, almost as if he were spot-lighted for her, she perceived the Earl and standing beside him Mr. Archer.

Then two gentlemen began to clap and others cried out: "Bravo!" as they had before, and one said in a loud voice:

"The goddess has returned from Olympus! Let us hope she does not recognise us for the swine we undoubtedly are!"

There was a roar of laughter at this, but Ilouka did not turn her head as she moved forward, fixing her eyes on Mr. Archer.

He walked to meet her, took her hand in his, and raised it to his lips.

"Thank you for coming," he said in a low voice that only she could hear.

She knew then that she had been right in thinking it was important.

Still holding her hand, he drew her towards the Earl.

"M'Lord," he said, "may I present *Mademoiselle* Ilouka!"

She dropped the Earl a graceful curtsey, and the Earl said in the deep voice she had heard when she was trying to sleep:

"I am delighted to meet you, and of course I want to thank you for a very brilliant performance."

"You are very kind."

When she had risen from her curtsey she looked up into the Earl's eyes and found he was staring at her in a manner that somehow made her feel more shy than she was already.

She had been right in thinking that he was overwhelming and insufferably superior.

But she was determined not to give him the satisfaction of letting him think that he intimidated her.

"I have been admiring your house, My Lord," she said in the tone her mother would have used on such occasions, "and although I have often heard of your superlative horses, I did not realise you also owned such outstanding paintings."

She thought that for the moment she had surprised him, but he replied almost without a pause:

"I hope I may have the pleasure of showing them to you, *Mademoiselle*, but now my friends are anxious to meet you."

While she had been talking to the Earl, Ilouka realised that his guests had crowded round her.

Because there were so many of them and their faces were red and their eyes appraised her in a manner which she felt was impertinent, they seemed almost to be menacing her.

Without really meaning to, she took a step away from them, which took her to the Earl's side.

As if he understood, he said:

"I think, gentlemen, it would be rather embarrassing for *Mademoiselle* Ilouka to meet you all at once. It would be easier if I introduced you one by one, so that you each have a chance of conversing with her."

"I would prefer to dance with her!" one man replied, and another of the gentlemen retorted:

"That is only because you want to get your arms round her, Alec."

As this was a way Ilouka knew no gentleman would have spoken in her mother's Drawing-Room, she stiffened.

Because she suddenly had no wish to be left all alone with men who she thought had been drinking too much and were still holding glasses of wine in their hands, she said to the Earl:

"I am somewhat tired, My Lord. We have been travelling for two days, and I would prefer, if it is possible, to talk to you alone."

As she spoke she thought it might be the one opportunity she would have fo putting in a good word for Mr. Archer.

"The choice of course, is yours," the Earl replied, "and what I am going to suggest is that we sit down on the sofa before I offer you a glass of champagne."

As he spoke he indicated the sofa which was at the side of the fireplace, and Ilouka immediately walked towards it to seat herself so that she faced the room.

There was a table covered with exquisite pieces of china directly behind her, so it was impossible for any of the guests to approach her unawares.

It was almost as if they had become a threatening pack of wolves, and only by avoiding direct contact with them could she feel safe.

As she was speaking to the Earl she had noticed that Mr. Archer had deliberately moved away.

He knew he was not wanted and tactfully had walked to where at the other end of the room stood a large and impressive piano.

He sat down and began to play very softly the sort of music which would make a suitable background to conversation without intruding on it.

As the Earl joined Ilouka on the sofa, she heard his guests making remarks to the effect that it was no use competing against Vincent, while another said:

"I never bet on the favourite."

They were certainly laughing and joking amongst themselves because they thought that the Earl was monopolising her.

At the same time, she had the feeling that they were too much in awe of him both as a man and as their host to protest about it.

As the Earl sat down beside her he said:

"Did you say you would like a glass of champagne, or would you prefer a liqueur?"

"I want nothing, thank you," Ilouka replied, "except to hear that you enjoyed our entertainment tonight."

"I thought that there would be no need for me to express the obvious."

"Then you were pleased?" Ilouka insisted.

"Far more pleased than I could possibly have anticipated."

She gave him a smile before she said:

"I am glad, so very glad!"

"Why?" the Earl enquired abruptly.

"Because it means a great deal to Mr. Archer," Ilouka said. "Like many people in the theatrical world, he has been going through a very difficult time, and your request for an entertainment here this evening came at just the right moment for him."

She paused, and as the Earl did not speak she bent forward to say pleadingly:

"Please ask him to come here another time, and perhaps you will tell your friends how good he is."

The Earl raised his eye-brows.

He was sitting sideways so that he faced her rather than leaning against the back of the sofa, and there was an expression on his face that she did not understand as he said:

"I thought we were talking about you."

"I am of no importance," Ilouka said quickly, "and as Mr. Archer made clear, I am here to give one performance and one only. But for him it is different . . ."

She could not say more because the Earl interrupted her to ask:

"Where in London are you performing? And why have I not seen you?"

For a second Ilouka hesitated, wondering what she should reply.

Then she said a little mockingly:

"I thought Mr. Archer made it quite clear that I was

here to amuse you before I returned to the place from
whence I came."

"And where is that place?"

"Where could it be but Olympus?"

She thought she was being rather clever in preventing
him from being too inquisitive, but the Earl said:

"You cannot expect me to be content with such an
imprecise address, but it is something we can talk about
later."

"I want to help Mr. Archer."

"Why? What does he mean to you?" the Earl enquired.

"I am sorry for him."

As she spoke she thought that perhaps she had taken
the wrong line.

The Earl might be the type of man who liked success
and was interested in obtaining only the best.

Perhaps, she thought, in trying to help Mr. Archer
she might have done him a disservice, in that the Earl,
with all his money, would wish to employ only those
entertainers who could command a large audience and
a high fee elsewhere.

Because she felt so deeply concerned for Mr. Archer
she said quickly:

"He is not begging for himself, but I am aware that
because you are so important in sporting and in the
Social World, you could do much to help him."

She thought there was a cynical twist to the Earl's
lips as he said:

"Most young women in your position want me to
help them."

"I am in no need of help," Ilouka said quickly.

"Are you sure of that?"

"Very, very sure."

"Are you now speaking as a goddess, or as an aspiring
young dancer whom I have not yet seen on the stage at
Covent Garden, which would be a far more prestigious
place for you to perform than at the Royal Olympic
Theatre?"

There was silence while Ilouka wondered what she could answer, and the Earl went on:

"I presume that you are intending to remain with Madame Vestris when the next Season opens. I consider you are wasted as an understudy, and I could promise to find you a part in a very much more important Theatre where I can undoubtedly arrange for you to play a lead."

"That is very kind of you," Ilouka replied, "but I was not asking you to help me, but Mr. Archer."

"Why is he so important to you? Or let me put the question I asked you just now in a different way: why are you so concerned about him?"

It flashed through Ilouka's mind that perhaps the Earl thought he was a relative of hers or that in some way she was indebted to him.

Because she had no wish to lie, and at the same time she wished to try to make the Earl understand why she wanted to help Mr. Archer, she hesitated before she said:

"I am sure you are finding this conversation very boring, My Lord. Let us talk about something more interesting."

"I want to talk about you," he replied.

"I would rather talk about horses, and Apollo in particular. How is he?"

"What do you know about my horses? This is the second time you have mentioned them."

"I know how sucessful you have been on the racecourse," Ilouka answered, "and I remember when you won the Derby with Apollo what a magnificent race it was, and how in fact he only won by a nose."

As she spoke she recalled her father describing it to her and saying it was the most exciting race he had ever watched.

"I did not even mind losing my money, which I can ill-afford," he had said to her mother, "because I wanted the best horse to win, and it was not until the very last second that we were aware which one that was."

"*I* mind you losing it, darling," her mother had replied, "because we cannot afford losses, however small."

"Do you know how much I lost in the whole day's racing?" her father had asked.

Her mother shook her head and Ilouka was aware of the look of anxiety in her beautiful eyes.

"Nothing!" her father laughed. "In fact, I won!"

He had taken a large handful of notes and coins from his pocket and put them into her mother's lap.

"My lovely doubting Thomas does not trust me!" he said. "But I return to you on this occasion the winner!"

"Oh, darling, I am glad," her mother replied.

Her father had laughed and pulled his wife into his arms, forgetting that the money was in her lap.

The coins had rolled all over the floor and Ilouka picked them up.

As she did so she thought how it made everybody happy when her father won when he gambled, but unhappy when he lost.

It was the same with people, she thought now, and while the Earl might worry about his horses, he did not understand how much the losers in life suffered.

"If you do not leave too early tomorrow morning," he was saying, "which is something I hope I can persuade you not to do, I will show you Apollo."

"He is here?"

"Yes, he is here, and actually he ran in a race today, heavily handicapped, but he won."

"Oh, I am so glad!" Ilouka exclaimed. "I would love to see him! It would be very thrilling for me."

She spoke with such excitement in her voice that the Earl looked at her curiously.

She was aware that if she could see Apollo it would make her feel close to her father, as in the days when he would describe to her in the evening the races he had watched and explain how the winner had managed to beat the rest of the field.

"Is the fact that I have a horse in which you are

interested the reason why you agreed to come here?"
the Earl asked. "I was certainly not expecting anybody
quite so talented, or quite so beautiful."

He spoke in a dry, rather cold manner which did not
make the compliment embarrassing.

Because he had asked her a direct question, Ilouka
answered truthfully:

"When I agreed to come here with Mr. Archer," she
said, "I was not aware that you were the owner of
Apollo, because when he won the Derby your name
was Hampton."

"I am very flattered that you should be interested in
me," the Earl said. "At the same time, I cannot believe
that you were very old at the time of that particular
race, nor were you appearing in any London Theatre,
or I would have seen you."

"That is true," Ilouka answered.

"How old are you?"

Ilouka saw no reason to lie and replied:

"I am just eighteen."

"When did you join Madame Vestris at the Royal
Olympic Theatre?"

Ilouka was thinking quickly what she should reply,
when they were interrupted by one of the Earl's guests.

He was obviously older than the Earl himself. In fact,
Ilouka thought, he was almost middle-aged. His face
was not only red but somewhat puffy under the eyes,
which gave him the debauched look that she found
repugnant.

"You are being distinctly unfair, Vincent," he said as
he stood beside the Earl at the sofa. "You are behaving
like a dog in a manger, and if you are not careful you
will have a revolution on your hands."

The Earl smiled.

"I am sorry, George," he said, "but as you will
understand, I find *Mademoiselle* Ilouka absorbingly interesting, and I have no wish to surrender my position
to anybody else."

"Well, I think it is too bad," his friend expostulated.

"Very well," the Earl said with a sigh. "*Mademoiselle*, may I present Lord Marlowe, a gentleman who will flatter you outrageously, so I suggest you take everything he says to you with the proverbial 'pinch of salt'!"

As he spoke the Earl from the sofa, and because Ilouka had no wish to talk to Lord Marlowe, who she was quite certain had drunk far too much, she also rose.

"I hope, My Lord," she said, "you will not think it rude if I retire. I am in fact feeling exhausted."

"Now that I cannot allow," Lord Marlowe said. "I want to talk to you, lovely lady, and I have a lot of things to whisper into those pretty little ears of yours which will be greatly to your advantage to hear."

As he spoke he put out his hand to touch her, but Ilouka looked at the Earl and said:

"I would like to say good-night to Mr. Archer, then go to bed."

She did not wait for his approval or for the words which Lord Marlowe was already beginning to say to her.

She moved swiftly across the room with a grace that made everybody she passed stand watching her until she reached the piano.

D'Arcy Archer looked at her from the piano-stool, then lifted his fingers from the keyboard.

"I want to go to bed," Ilouka said quickly in a low voice.

"I am sorry," he said, "but they insisted upon your coming downstairs and there was nothing I could do about it."

"I understand," she said. "Now, please, may I go?"

"It will not be easy . . ." D'Arcy Archer began, then was silent as the Earl joined them.

"I have an idea to which I hope you will agree," he said as D'Arcy Archer rose to his feet.

"What is that, My Lord?"

"It is that you stay with me tomorrow and give another performance for my dinner-party tomorrow evening."

Ilouka wished to say that was impossible, but she saw the delight in Mr. Archer's eyes as he realised what the Earl had asked.

"I have in fact," the Earl continued, "engaged another type of entertainment to amuse my guests, but I feel sure there is nothing they would enjoy more than a repetition of your performance, or a variation of what occurred this evening. I assure you I will be very generous for taking up so much of your time."

"Your proposition is something which I shall be only too delighted to accept, My Lord," D'Arcy Archer replied, "but of course, I first have to have the agreement of *Mademoiselle*."

He looked at Ilouka as he spoke, and she knew that he was pleading with her, begging her almost on his knees to agree.

"You have already told me," the Earl said to Ilouka, "that you would like to see Apollo, and I would enjoy showing you the rest of my stable. We could make the visit tomorrow morning before I leave with my friends for the races at about noon. And while I am away, the house and gardens are at your disposal, and those too I think you will find of interest."

As he spoke Ilouka was thinking that if she behaved as she ought to, she would refuse the Earl's invitation and insist on Mr. Archer taking her to where she could find a Stage-Coach to carry her to Bedfordshire.

But if she did that, she knew she would feel that she was being cruel in depriving Mr. Archer of the opportunity he craved so fervently. It would be a selfish act which would be of no real benefit to herself.

Strange and unusual though this party was, reprehensible though it might be for her to be alone with a large number of gentlemen, some of whom had undoubtedly imbibed too freely, to her mind it was certainly preferable to sitting in the ugly, stiff Drawing-Room at Stone House and being nagged by Aunt Agatha.

Both men were waiting for her decision, and she had

the feeling that the Earl was very confident that he would get his own way and she would not refuse him.

Because she thought there was a smile of victory on his lips and an expression of triumph in his eyes, she longed to say "no."

But one glance at Mr. Archer decided her.

Once again there was that pleading spaniel look on his face that made her feel he was very pathetic.

"It would be a pity," she said slowly, "if after pleasing Your Lordship tonight we disappointed you tomorrow."

"I am quite certain you will not do that," the Earl replied, "and anyway, let us say it is a risk I am prepared to take."

Now he was definitely smiling, and as she thought it annoyed her she said:

"Very well, I agree to do what Your Lordship wishes, but I would still like to retire now."

"Then I will allow you to do that," the Earl answered, "but before you go will you agree to sing once again for my friends, who are feeling upset at enjoying so little of your company? I would be extremely grateful if you would oblige me."

He looked at D'Arcy Archer as he spoke, and Ilouka knew that without saying so he would be ready to pay for the extra song.

"It will not be too much for you?" D'Arcy Archer asked as he seated himself once more at the piano.

Ilouka knew he was elated at the success she had been, and most of all at the thought of staying another night and earning more money.

"No, I am all right," Ilouka replied. "What am I to sing?"

"Sing a song they know well," he suggested.

He lowered his voice and added:

"By this time, after such a good dinner, they will appreciate almost anything! So do not be nervous."

"I am not, as it happens," Ilouka answered.

As she spoke she saw Lord Marlowe staring at her and realised that while they had been talking to the

Earl he had come up the room and moved until he was quite near to the piano.

The Earl turned to his friends.

"Gentlemen, I have persuaded *Mademoiselle* Ilouka to sing us a good-night song, and she had also promised to entrance us again tomorrow evening with her dancing."

There was a murmur of approval at this, and without waiting any longer D'Arcy Archer struck the first chord of the Bavarian Girls' song *Bring My Broom*.

Ilouka stood beside him at the piano, and as she did so she saw the Earl move towards the door, open it, and speak to a footman on duty outside.

She wondered if he was not interested in hearing her sing, but even before the piano introduction had finished he had shut the door again and was leaning against the wall beside it as the song started.

As it was a sprightly German tune, Ilouka realised it appealed to the audience as Mr. Archer had expected it to do.

When she finished, there was a burst of applause which started even before she curtseyed.

Then as she smiled at Mr. Archer and they moved towards the door, Lord Marlowe was at her side.

"That, *Mademoiselle*, was quite entrancing! And I want to have the opportunity of telling you so," he said in a thick voice.

He would have taken her hand, but Ilouka managed to avoid him, and before he could prevent her from doing so, she sped towards the door where the Earl was holding it open, waiting for her.

"Good-night!" she said as she reached him.

The Earl followed her out into the Hall and shut the door of the Salon behind him.

"I enjoyed your singing," he said, "but your dancing is something very different—so different that I cannot think why you have not been discovered before now."

"You are very complimentary, My Lord," Ilouka said, "but actually, although you may find this hard to believe,

I have no wish to be discovered and am quite happy as I am."

"Are you telling me," he asked as they walked towards the staircase, "that you are not infatuated, entranced, and obsessed about the stage, which you have chosen as your career?"

"I think the answer is," Ilouka replied, "that I do not particularly want to do anything but be myself, and to express myself in my own way."

As she spoke she thought she had been very clever.

She had not lied, she had told the truth, and if he put a different construction on what she was saying, that was not her problem.

But she was aware as they reached the bottom of the staircase that he was looking at her penetratingly and searchingly, as if he thought she had a reason for being elusive and was determined to find out what it was.

She held out her hand and curtseyed.

"Good-night, My Lord."

He did not reply, but took her hand in his and held it for a moment while his grey eyes were still searching her face.

She looked up at him and something frivolous that she had been about to say died on her lips. Instead, she could only look at him, feeling that he had something important to say to her, but she had no idea what it was.

Then because she heard the sound of voices and laughter coming from behind them and knew the Salon door had opened again, she took her hand from the Earl's clasp and without saying any more hurried up the stairs.

She did not look back, although she knew he had not moved from where she had left him.

"I am puzzling him," she told herself. "He must not become too inquisitive, but it will do him good to know that I am different in a way he cannot explain."

She walked up the staircase, but when she would

have turned left, towards the room she occupied, an elderly housemaid appeared.

"Excuse me, Miss," she said, "but I have had to move you to another room."

"Move me?" Ilouka enquired. "But . . . why?"

"His Lordship felt you were not as comfortable as you could be," the housemaid replied. "Come this way, Miss, and I'll show you where you are sleeping now."

Ilouka thought it was rather strange, for actually the room in which she had been hand seemed very comfortable.

She followed the housemaid along a passage towards another part of the great house.

They walked for some way until the housemaid opened a door to a room which was very much larger, more impressive, and certainly more beautiful than the one she had occupied.

The room was exactly what she would have expected the State-Room of an early Georgian house to be.

It had a painted ceiling, panelled walls, long windows draped with fringed pelmets, and a beautiful four-poster bed, carved and gilded, with curtains of silk embroidered skilfully in a manner which Ilouka knew would send her mother into ecstasies.

She wanted to ask questions as to why her room had been changed, and as she was about to do so she saw that there were two housemaids in the room hanging up her gowns that had previously been unpacked and that her two trunks were there too.

She decided it would be wrong to ask questions in the circumstances and could only say:

"I would be grateful if you would undo my gown. I am very tired, and I am sure I shall sleep peacefully."

"I certainly hope so, Miss," the housemaid said in a voice that seemed almost an echo of Hannah's.

The thought of her old maid brought her back so vividly that Ilouka somehow thought she was there, disapproving strongly of the way she was behaving, and even more so because she had agreed to repeat the same reprehensible act tomorrow.

"Poor, dear Hannah!" Ilouka murmured beneath her breath, as the housemaid undid her gown and hung it up in the wardrobe.

Another housemaid showed her that opening out of the bedroom was a sunken bath similar to the drawings she had seen of Roman baths.

"How extraordinary to find one here in a Georgian house!" she exclaimed.

"His Lordship had it built in what was originally a Powder-Closet," the housemaid explained again, in a somewhat disapproving voice, "but most ladies prefer to bathe in their bedrooms, as is usual."

Ilouka wanted to laugh, knowing how servants always disliked anything different and out of the ordinary.

She thought that while she was staying with the Earl she would certainly avail herself of his modern innovations, whatever they might be.

The housemaids curtseyed and went from the room, and when they had gone Ilouka went to the door to turn the key in the lock.

The last words her mother had said to her before she left for her journey to Bedfordshire had been:

"I only hope, dearest, that the Inn where you will stay the night is not too uncomfortable, and do not forget to lock the door securely. If it has a weak and ineffective lock, put a chair under the handle."

Ilouka had smiled.

"I will remember, Mama, but I think it unlikely that robbers will creep in to steal anything from me."

"It is not only robbers who might disturb you, darling," Lady Armstrong had replied. "So promise you will not forget."

"Of course I promise, Mama. Do not worry," Ilouka had said. "I will lock my door, say my prayers, and not forget to clean my teeth."

She had laughed as she spoke, and Lady Armstrong

had put her arms round her to say, almost as if she spoke to herself:

"You are far too lovely, my precious one, to be travelling about the country in Stage-Coaches instead of in a private carriage with two men on the box."

"I shall be safe enough," Ilouka had replied. "I cannot believe that even the stupidest farm yokel would think I would make him a competent wife and begin to pursue me ardently with Hannah's full disapproval."

Lady Armstrong had laughed again.

"That is true enough, darling. At the same time, I am worried, so do not forget everything I have told you."

Ilouka had kissed her mother good-bye and thought as they drove away that she was being needlessly apprehensive.

It was unlikely that anything so eventful as thieves, robbers, or highwaymen would trouble her while Hannah was there.

Instead, she had dropped dramatically into the most fantastic adventure she could possible have imagined.

"I certainly never expected to sleep in a room like this," she said to herself.

She washed in the Roman bath, which also had an elegant wash-hand-stand with hot water in a polished brass can which was covered with a quilted cosy to keep it warm.

Then she blew out the candles, except for two by her bed, and knelt down to say her prayers.

She prayed for Hannah and the poor actress who had died beside her, she thanked God for what had been a very exciting evening, and she prayed that the Earl would be kind to Mr. Archer after they had left Lavenham House.

Lastly, Ilouka prayed that she would be forgiven for the lies she had told and for doing something of which she knew her mother would not approve.

"But I am sure she would also think it wrong not to help poor Mr. Archer," she said.

As she finished her prayers she thought it would be

nice if one could ever hear the answers to the questions
one asked, then decided it would be very disconcerting
if one did.

She took a last glance round the room and got into
bed.

As she had expected, the mattress was very soft and
comfortable, the pillows were filled with the finest
down, and the sheets were of finer linen than she had
ever slept in before.

'His Lordship certainly lives in comfort,' she thought.

For a moment she did not blow out the candles
because the room was so beautiful and she wanted to
look at it, picturing the Countesses who had slept there
in the past.

She wondered if the Earl's guests had ever included
Queen Adelaide, for this room was certainly fit for a
Queen.

Then unexpectedly, surprisingly, when everything was
quiet, she heard a knock on the door.

It was very faint, and she thought for the moment
she must be mistaken, until it came again.

As she listened she wondered if it was a housemaid
who had returned because something had been forgotten.

But before she could decide whether or not to ask
who was there, she heard a voice which she recognised
say:

"Let me in, pretty lady. I want to speak to you."

Ilouka sat upright in bed.

It was Lord Marlowe! There was no mistaking the
thick voice in which he had spoken to her before, only
now it seemed even more slurred.

"Let me in!" he said. "I must talk to you! I insist!"

Quite suddenly Ilouka was frightened, more frightened than she had ever been before in her life.

She leapt out of bed to run to the door and look at
the lock.

She touched it and it seemed that because it was so
large it would be strong and secure.

But as the handle turned and returned she realised

that Lord Marlowe was putting pressure on the door from outside, and she had the terrifying feeling that it would give.

She looked round frantically and saw a chair painted white and gold with a brocade seat. Dragging it to the door, she fixed the frame under the handle as her mother had told her to do.

Her heart was beating frantically in case Lord Marlowe should break in, and she was frightened to the point where she wanted to scream, but she knew it would be useless.

The room where she knew Mr. Archer was sleeping was a long way away, and she had the idea that even if she screamed no-one would be interested, except for Lord Marlowe, who would renew his efforts to reach her.

There was an armchair on which the maid had placed her dressing-gown.

It was quite heavy, but by using all her strength Ilouka managed to push it over the carpet towards the door, but now Lord Marlowe was not whispering and his voice had grown louder as he said:

"Let me in! Let me in!"

She thought, although being so inexperienced she could not be sure, that he was too drunk to know when he was beaten and too befuddled to move away.

She gave the armchair another push, still hoping it would hold the door closed.

Then as she wondered frantically what else she should do, the door on the other side of the fireplace, which she had not noticed before, opened and the Earl entered the room.

She turned her head and saw him there, and with a leap of her heart she knew he had come to save her.

"Please . . . please . . . help me!" she cried before he could speak. "If the lock breaks . . . Lord Marlowe will be able to . . . come in."

She was not aware of what she was saying, she was

only concerned that the Earl seemed like an angel of deliverance, there when she least expected it.

Then she saw the expression of anger on his face.

"I will deal with this!" he said, and left the room by the door through which he had come.

Chapter Five

Ilouka stood clasping her hands together and listening.

She could still hear Lord Marlowe's voice and he was still pushing against the door.

Although she knew now that even if he did burst in the Earl would save her, at the same time without realising it she was holding her breath until she heard his voice.

Then it came, and although she could not hear exactly what he said, she realised from his tone that he was being sharp and commanding.

She could hear Lord Marlowe expostulating. His voice was raised so that she could have heard what he was saying, but she was no longer listening.

Instead, she was standing dazed and immobile until finally she heard Lord Marlowe, grumbling and protesting but moving away until his voice faded altogether.

Then she turned round to look towards the door by which the Earl had entered her room.

Vaguely at the back of her mind she supposed there must be a Sitting-Room attached to her bedroom as there was in the room she had first been given.

She had little time to think before the Earl came back, and she thought as he walked towards her that he seemed taller and more omnipotent than he had seemed in the Dining-Room.

She thought perhaps it was because he was wearing

not his evening-clothes but a dark robe which almost reached the floor.

When he came to her side, she had intended to thank him.

Instead, perhaps because of the relief she felt that he had saved her from Lord Marlowe, or perhaps because she had not been exaggerating when she said she was very tired, she felt the room begin to swim round her.

She put out her hand to hold on to the Earl to prevent herself from falling.

"Are you all right?" he asked.

"I . . . I was so . . . frightened," Ilouka said incoherently.

"You have had a long day . . . "

He picked her up in her arms, carried her to bed, and put her down against the pillows.

As he did so, far away at the back of her mind Ilouka thought he must think her very foolish, but it did not seem to matter.

"Go to sleep," the Earl said, "and I will say what I want to say another time."

She wondered vaguely what that could be, but was really too exhausted to ask questions.

Then she knew that the Earl had moved from her bedside and was pulling the armchair back to its proper place from where she had pushed it against the door.

He also moved back the chair she had placed there first.

"Y-you . . . do not think . . . Lord Marlowe will come- . . . back?" she asked.

"You may be certain he will not do that," the Earl answered.

"He is . . . horrible!" Ilouka murmured. "And he . . . has had too . . . much to . . . dri . . . "

The last words faded away into silence, and the Earl placed the chair with the brocade seat down beside the bed and stood looking at Ilouka.

Her hair was falling over the pillow and over her shoulders, and as it caught the light from the candles it seemed to glow as if with little flames.

Her eye-lashes were very dark against her cheeks and she looked very young, child-like, and vulnerable.

The Earl stood looking at her for a long time, realising from the rhythmic rise and fall of her breast that she was in a deep sleep.

Then with a faint smile he bent forward and kissed her very gently on the lips.

Ilouka made a little movement but she did not wake.

The Earl picked up one of the candles beside the bed, blew out the other, and went from the room, closing the communicating door behind him.

* * *

Ilouka came back to consciousness feeling as if she moved through layers and layers of sleep until she was aware that there was a light in the room and the maid was pulling back the curtains.

For a moment she could not remember where she was and thought she must be at home.

Then as she clutched at her dreams as if they were precious, she suddenly remembered everything that had happened the day before.

She was not at The Towers but was staying with the Earl of Lavenham and was supposed to be an understudy for Madame Vestris at the Royal Olympic Theatre in London.

It seemed even more ridiculous than any of her dreams had ever been. Then she opened her eyes wide and as she did so the maid came to the bedside to say:

"Excuse me, Miss, for disturbing you, but His Lordship'll be leaving for the races in a short while and wishes to speak to you before he goes."

Ilouka sat up in bed.

"What time is it?"

"After eleven o'clock, Miss."

"Oh no! It cannot be!" Ilouka exclaimed in dismay.

She remembered that the Earl had promised to show

her Apollo and his other horses, and by oversleeping she had missed seeing them.

Then she remembered that she and Mr. Archer were to stay another night and there was therefore every chance that she could see them tomorrow.

"How could I have slept so late?" she asked aloud.

"I expects you were tired, Miss," the maid replied. "I've brought your breakfast."

As she spoke she carried a tray to the side of the bed and set it down on the table.

"Thank you," Ilouka said.

"Shall I fill the sunken bath, Miss," the maid enquired, "or would you prefer one here in your bedroom?"

Ilouka smiled.

"I am longing to use the Roman bath," she replied. "I have never been in one before."

"Very good, Miss."

She spoke in a tone which told Ilouka she thought it would be far more proper if she bathed in her bedroom.

'Hannah would have felt the same,' Ilouka thought, and felt a pang of grief for the old maid.

It was Hannah's death that had prevented her from sleeping the previous night, which had made her miss seeing Apollo.

Besides which, although she had not been aware of it, the singing and dancing in front of an audience of strangers had been a strain that she had never encountered before.

And heaped upon it had been her fear, which had amounted to terror when Lord Marlowe had tried to force her bedroom door open.

'Thank goodness the Earl came to save me when he did!' she thought, and wondered how he knew what was happening.

She supposed that he slept nearby and must have heard Lord Marlowe pleading with her to let him in.

"How could he imagine I would do such a thing?" Ilouka asked herself indignantly.

She supposed that when men had drunk too much

they had strange ideas and behaved in a way which they would not do in ordinary circumstances.

She ate her breakfast, which was delicious, and there was also a peach which she knew must have come from a hothouse.

She thought as she peeled it that it was a mistake to stay another night here, comfortable though it might be.

She had helped Mr. Archer because she had been sorry for him, but he had in fact said that she was appearing for one performance and one performance only.

Tonight she would be forced to meet Lord Marlowe again, or at least to be aware that he was watching her and trying to attract her attention as he had done last night.

"Mama would be horrified!" Ilouka told herself. "If I behaved properly, I would go away today."

Even as she thought of it she knew she could not be so cruel as to let down Mr. Archer when he was so thrilled by the Earl's appreciation of the entertainment he had provided for him.

"I shall just ignore Lord Marlowe," Ilouka told herself. "In any case, I want to see the horses, and I also find it interesting to talk to the Earl."

He might be slightly superior, but he had certainly used that quality to her advantage when he had sent Lord Marlowe away from her door.

Thinking back, she remembered how he had tidied the room so that the housemaids would not think it strange when they called her in the morning.

She supposed that the maid had come in through the Sitting-Room as he had, as she had not awakened in time to unlock the door to the passage.

'He was very kind,' Ilouka thought.

She remembered that he had lifted her into bed, and for the first time she was aware that while she had been pushing the furniture in front of the door to keep out

Lord Marlowe she had been wearing only a thin nightgown.

It fastened at the neck and had little frills over her wrists. At the same time, because it was of such fine lawn it must have appeared almost transparent.

She felt herself blushing to think that a strange man had seen her so immodestly garbed.

"I do not suppose he noticed," Ilouka comforted herself.

It was difficult to remember what he had said or if she had thanked him before he left.

He must have blown out the candles, and vaguely, so that it was difficult to put into a coherent idea, she thought that he had said something which had made her heart leap before she had finally faded away into the deepest depths of sleep.

'What can it have been?' she wondered.

Then she knew it could not have been anything the Earl said but was part of her dream in which she thought that somebody had touched her lips, and she had been kissed for the first time in her life.

'That would be a dream,' she thought; but it was different from any dream she had dreamt before.

She finished the peach, jumped out of bed, and went into the closet where the sunken Roman bath was.

Two maids were pouring into it cans of hot water. There was another of cold water in case the bath should be too hot, then they left her to bathe herself.

It was exciting to step down the three marble steps into the bath and sit below the surface, feeling as if she had slipped back into the past and was the daughter of a Roman General or perhaps the Emperor himself.

'I must tell Mama about this,' she thought, and wondered if she would ever dare to do so.

She did not linger long, knowing that the Earl was waiting. Back in the bedroom, the maid helped her dress and she put on a very pretty gown of pale green muslin sprigged with tiny flowers.

The material had come from Paris and had been

made for her by one of the Royal dressmakers in London, and only when she had glanced at herself in the mirror did she think that she looked far too richly gowned to be an actress who had to earn her own living.

However, it was too late to change, and she said to the maid:

"Where will I find His Lordship?"

"He is waiting for you, Miss, in the *Boudoir* next door."

Ilouka had expected him to be downstairs and was embarrassed because it somehow seemed so intimate.

The maid opened the communicating door and she went into the *Boudoir*.

It was far bigger than she had expected, and far more impressive. The walls were hung with exquisite French paintings, the furniture was French, and there was the fragrance of carnations which filled several vases.

The Earl was sitting in a comfortable chair, reading a newspaper.

He put it down and rose as Ilouka walked into the room, and as she saw his eyes glance at her gown, she thought he was aware that it was not suitable for the role in which she appeared.

"Good-morning... My Lord," she said hastily. "I am very... upset that I overslept... and I must... apologise. It is my loss, because I was so looking forward to seeing Apollo."

"I have something to tell you," the Earl said quietly, "and I am afraid it will come as rather a shock."

"A ... shock?" Ilouka repeated in surprise.

"I suggest you sit down."

She looked at him wonderingly, trying to guess why he was speaking in such a grave tone.

At the same time, she could not help admiring the elegance with which he was dressed, and she saw that in the daylight he seemed if anything to be better-looking than he had the night before.

Because he was obviously waiting for her to sit, she

did so obediently, but she raised her eyes to his apprehensively, wondering what he could be about to say.

She was suddenly afraid that by some terrible mischance he had discovered who she was.

"What I have to tell you," the Earl said very quietly, "is that when Mr. Archer was called this morning by the footman who was valeting him, it was found that he had died during the night."

For a moment it was impossible for Ilouka to take in what the Earl had said.

Then she exclaimed:

"What are you . . . saying? It . . . cannot be . . . true!"

"I am afraid it is," the Earl said. "After all, he was I think a very old man. Perhaps he suffered from heart trouble and was not aware of it, but I think it will be some consolation for you to know that he died with a smile on his lips."

"I cannot . . . believe it!" Ilouka said. "He was so happy to . . . come here, and so very . . . happy that you asked him to stay . . . another night."

The Earl sat down beside her on the sofa. Then he said in a rather different tone of voice:

"What did this man mean to you?"

"I was so sorry for him," Ilouka replied. "He told me this was his . . . last chance and unless he could . . . please you he faced . . . starvation."

"Is that the only reason you came with him?"

"He pleaded with me and begged me to save him, and I thought it would be cruel to say 'No' . . . "

"I had a feeling it must be something like that," the Earl said.

"It does not seem . . . possible that he is . . . dead."

As she spoke Ilouka was thinking that Hannah always said that things happened in threes, and on this occasion it was certainly true.

Three deaths in a row, Hannah's, Lucille Ganymede's, and now poor Mr. Archer's.

She was aware that the Earl was watching her face, and after a moment she said:

"Perhaps in a way it was the... best way for him to... die. He knew he had been a success last night, and you had asked him to give another performance, and that meant he would have enough... money to last him for a... long time."

"That is a very sensible way to look at it," the Earl said. "I want you to leave everything to me, Ilouka. I will see that he is buried in the Churchyard in the Park, and unless you particularly wish to do so, I see no point in your upsetting yourself by being present at his Funeral. But of course, you will wish to notify his relatives."

"I do not know... who they are."

"You mean you only know this man professionally?"

Without thinking, she told the truth.

"I met him only the day before yesterday."

As she spoke she realised she had made a mistake, because the Earl said:

"When he asked you to come here?"

There was a little pause.

"Yes... that was it," Ilouka agreed.

"Then I think we can leave notification of his death to the Agent who was contacted by my secretary," the Earl said. "It was he who arranged the entertainment for my party, and he will pay any money Archer has left to those depending on him."

As he finished speaking the Earl smiled at Ilouka and added:

"That leaves you to be provided for, and I want you to have no worries on that score. I will look after you."

"Thank you," Ilouka said quickly, "but I..."

She had been about to say that there was no need for anybody to look after her, when the Earl rose to his feet, took her hand, and pulled her to her feet.

"Now listen, Ilouka," he said, "we have a great deal to say to each other, you and I, but now I have to leave with my friends for the races. I want you to stay here, explore the house, walk in the garden, and rest until I return."

"But . . . I think I . . . ought to . . . go away," Ilouka managed to say.

The Earl smiled again.

"Do you really think I would let you do that?" he asked. "I intend to protect you and prevent you from getting into this sort of trouble again."

Ilouka stared at him as if she could not believe what he was saying.

Then as she was trying to find words, he put his fingers under her chin and turned her face up to his.

Just for a moment he looked down into her eyes, then incredibly, so that she could hardly believe what was happening, his lips came down on hers.

Ilouka had never been kissed and she had no idea that a man's lips could make her feel as if she were his captive and it was impossible to try to escape.

For a moment she was too amazed, too astonished to even think clearly of what was happening.

When she told herself that she must struggle, she felt as if a streak of lightning swept through her body.

It was the strange ecstasy she had felt when she was dancing, which seemed to come from some music within her heart and which she felt must be in the Earl's heart too, and that they listened to it together.

It was so enthralling and so mesmeric that it seemed to pulsate through her, and even as she felt it moving within herself and flowing out in little waves, she knew that the same feeling came from him.

They were linked together not only by their lips but by every breath they drew and the life within themselves.

It was so rapturous, so ecstatic, that when the Earl raised his head she could only stare at him, her eyes seeming to fill her small face.

Her voice had died in her throat.

"Now do you understand?" he asked in a deep voice. "We will talk about it when I return. Until then, take care of yourself."

As he finished speaking he walked away and opened the door of the Sitting-Room, then went out and shut it behind him.

For a moment it was impossible for Ilouka to move.

She could only stand where he had left her, conscious that her heart was throbbing in her breast and her whole body was pulsating in a manner she had never known before.

It was an extension of the emotions she had felt last night when she had danced to the gypsy music and known that she was searching for love.

Then because it was so overwhelming, so unlike anything she had ever dreamt of or imagined, she sat down again on the sofa and covered her eyes with her hands.

She seemed to be sitting there for a long time.

Then gradually as the throbbing of her heart returned to normal and the rapture that was in her throat and in her breasts seemed to fade into the distance, she knew that she must face facts and try to be sensible.

She tried not to think of the wonder the Earl had aroused in her, and with some critical part of her brain she forced herself to think clearly.

She knew that what the Earl was saying was something which would shock and horrify her mother and to which it was impossible for her to listen.

She could hear Mr. Archer saying to her that Lucille Ganymede had lost her "Protector" and that was one reason why she was willing to come with him to entertain the Earl of Lavenham.

Ilouka had not realised exactly what the word "Protector" meant.

Now vaguely she remembered things her father had said which she had not understood at the time but which now became more clear.

He had not known she was listening when he had said to her mother on one occasion:

"Madame Vestris has fallen on her feet. She is under the protection of one of the richest men in London."

"I thought she was married," Mrs. Compton had replied.

"They have parted company," the Colonel answered, "which from Lucy Vestris's point of view is about the best thing that could happen to her financially."

"I cannot think why the affairs of such women interest you, darling," Mrs. Compton protested, and her husband laughed.

"If you are jealous, my love, there is no reason for it. I am just telling you the gossip of the Club. Living here, we usually get the news weeks or months later than anybody else."

Ilouka knew by the note in her father's voice that he was regretting once again, as he did so often, that they were too poor to spend much time in London and were unable to afford the sports that he found so engaging.

As if her mother thought the same thing, she quickly put her arms round her husband's neck and said:

"Oh, darling, I wish I were a rich heiress."

"In which case you would doubtless have married a Duke," the Colonel laughed, "and I would not have got a look in! I love you just as you are, and money is not really important where we are concerned."

"No, of course not," Mrs. Compton answered.

They had walked away with their arms round each other, unaware that Ilouka, sitting reading behind the curtain on the window-seat, had overheard what they said.

Not that she had been particularly interested at that time, but now she understood exactly what the Earl was offering her.

Moreover, it was not only a shock but positively frightening that his kiss had made her feel sensations she had not realised existed.

'I must go away!' she thought frantically. 'How can I stay here and go on deceiving him? How could I ever let him know that when he kissed me it was like dancing on the top of the snow-capped mountains?'

She thought that expressed all that she had felt.

Yet it was even more than that, for the feelings he had evoked in her were not as cold as snow, but warm and glowing like the sunshine, or perhaps the flames of a gypsy fire leaping higher and higher as she danced round it.

"I must go away!"

She repeated the words as if she forced herself to listen to them.

Yet as she rose to her feet she had an irrepressible desire to stay where she was and await the Earl's return from the races so that she could talk to him, and perhaps, although it was wrong to think it, he would kiss her again and she would feel the pressure of his lips on hers.

"I must be crazy!" Ilouka said to herself. "What...would Mama...think of me?"

She walked across the room to the window and as she did so she saw that she was looking out over the front of the house towards the lake and the Park.

To the left was the centre block of the building, and outside the front door she could see several Phaetons drawn up one behind the other, and she knew they were waiting to carry the Earl and his friends to the races.

As she watched, the gentlemen began to come out through the front door.

They stood for a moment on the steps, then the Earl was with them, his top-hat at the side of his dark head, his polished Hessian boots gleaming in contrast to the pale champagne-yellow of his tight-fitting pantaloons.

He stepped into the first Phaeton and one of his friends climbed in beside him.

A groom sprang up into the small seat behind, and when they moved off the Earl drove his horses in a way which told Ilouka that he was an expert with the reins.

The other vehicles were filled quickly with his friends, and those who had no wish to drive in a Phaeton travelled in a very comfortable and luxurious brake.

Ilouka stood at the window watching them until the

last sign of the cavalcade vanished beneath the thick foliage of the oak trees, then she gave a little sigh and went to her bedroom next door.

She knew that what she had to do was difficult, not only because she had never travelled alone before, but also, although she was ashamed to admit it, because her heart urged her to stay where she was.

* * *

Two hours later Ilouka was being driven down the drive.

She had given orders to the housemaids to pack for her and for a carriage to take her to the nearest Posting-Inn with an air of authority which prevented the servants from arguing or even suggesting that she should wait until their Master returned.

She was fortunate in that the Earl's secretary, who ran the house, had also gone to the races and there was therefore no-one of any real authority left behind to tell her what she should or should not do.

Only when she was dressed for travelling and her trunks were strapped and ready to go downstairs did she say to the Housekeeper:

"I would like to see Mr. Archer before I leave."

"Is that wise, Miss? It may upset you," the House-keeper replied.

"I would like to say a prayer beside him," Ilouka answered.

Without saying any more, the Housekeeper led her down a passage towards the room she had occupied when she first arrived.

The blinds were drawn, but there was enough light to see that Mr. Archer had been laid out with his hands crossed on his breast.

He looked, Ilouka thought as she neared the bed, almost as if he were carved in stone and lying on top of a tomb in a Church.

Now that she saw him dead, he looked younger, as if

there was no more for him to worry about, and the lines on his face were less deep-cut than they had been when he was alive.

The Earl had been right when he said he had died with a smile on his face, and he did in fact look happy.

'He *was* happy,' Ilouka thought.

She was certain that the Earl would not only have rewarded him well but recommended him to his friends.

But she knew his recommendation would not be of very much use unless Mr. Archer could ensure that the entertainment he provided would include herself.

Because the Earl had very different ideas on that score, it might have meant that when the money was spent, once again he would fall on ill times.

She knelt down beside the bed and said a prayer for his soul and asked that he would find peace.

As she rose to her feet she found herself thinking that perhaps God knew best, and Mr. Archer through his death had been saved a lot of misery and anxiety about a future in which every day he would be growing older.

She went out of the room to find that the House-keeper was waiting for her in the passage outside.

"The coffin'll be coming this afternoon for the poor gentleman," she said. "You'll not be staying for the Funeral, Miss?"

"I am afraid I cannot do that," Ilouka replied.

"If His Lordship wishes to get in touch with you, Miss, have you left an address?" the Housekeeper enquired.

"I think His Lordship knows all that is necessary," Ilouka replied evasively.

She thanked the Housekeeper, gave her a large tip for the housemaids who had looked after her, and thought she took it with surprise.

Then, going down the Grand Staircase, she knew she was saying good-bye to the most magnificent house she had ever seen, and also to the owner of it.

Only as she drove away did she think a little wistfully

that after all she had not seen Apollo, nor had she been able to explore all the rooms in the house.

"For the rest of my life I shall just have to imagine the things I did not see," she told herself.

But she knew she would not have to imagine what it was like to be kissed, and in future would understand what the poets were trying to say in their poems and the writers in their prose.

"How could I have been kissed by a man I had only just met, and who knew nothing about me?" she asked herself.

And yet his kiss had been more ecstatic, more rapturous, than anything she had imagined or read about.

When she reached the Posting-Inn she thanked the Earl's servants for driving her there, tipped both the coachman and the footman, again to their surprise, and ordered a Post-Chaise.

She thought that although it was unlikely, perhaps the Earl might try to trace her movements, and she therefore deliberately took the Post-Chaise only as far as the nearest town on the border of Bedfordshire.

She then changed vehicles, and after the conveyance which had taken her there drove away, she travelled on towards Stonefield village, in which Mrs. Adolphus's house was situated.

She felt that in that way she had covered her tracks both cleverly and successfully.

At the same time, she thought she was being extremely conceited in thinking that the Earl would be anxious to find her once she had gone or would make any effort to trace her.

'He must never know who I am,' she thought.

She wished Mr. Archer had not used her own Christian name when he had introduced her after the dinner-party, because that was the only clue the Earl might have to her identity.

"As far as he is concerned I am just an unimportant actress," Ilouka said aloud as she looked out from the Post-Chaise over the flat, dull fields of Bedfordshire.

He would return to the actress from Drury Lane and the beauties who pursued him relentlessly.

It was a pain like a dagger in her heart to think such things.

Then she told herself she was being ridiculous.

"I must remember that the Earl and Lord Marlowe are prepared to kiss any pretty women they meet."

She meant nothing serious in their lives. To them one woman was very like another.

'And yet to me he will always be different,' Ilouka thought.

Once again she felt that strange rapture moving within her, the music flooding from her heart, and the vibrations reaching out to touch the vibrations from the Earl and make them for one rapturous moment not two people but one.

'No wonder men and women seek for love all their lives,' Ilouka thought.

Then she started and felt that what she had thought was revolutionary because she had admitted to herself it was love.

* * *

"Riding alone in a Post-Chaise? I have never heard of such a thing!" Mrs. Adolphus exclaimed.

Ilouka had been ushered into the stiff, ugly Drawing-Room where she was seated in the window, a piece of embroidery in her hands.

"I had no alternative, Aunt Agatha," Ilouka replied. "There was an accident with the Stage-Coach, and poor Hannah was killed when it turned over."

Mrs. Adolphus stared at her as if she could not be speaking the truth.

Then she threw up her hands in horror to say:

"You travelled alone? How could you do such a thing?"

"What else could I do?" Ilouka answered. "It was only a small village and I do not suppose anyone there had ever heard of a lady's-maid, let alone having been trained as one."

"Surely there was something you could have done if you had taken any trouble over it," Mrs. Adolphus said, always ready to find fault. "And where did you stay the night, may I ask?"

"The Vicar was kind enough to give me a bedroom in the Vicarage," Ilouka replied.

She thought that at least that would sound highly respectable.

But Mrs. Adolphus asked cryptically:

"He was a married man?"

"No, but he was well over seventy-five, and his Housekeeper was an elderly woman and I promise you a most efficient Chaperone."

"There was nobody else with you?"

There was just a little pause before Ilouka knew that to tell the truth would be to evoke a thousand suspicions, so she answered:

"No . . . no-one else."

Mrs. Adolphus gave a sigh, not as if of relief but almost as if she was disappointed. Then she said:

"Well, you are here safely, although I must say I think your whole story is extremely bizarre, and I cannot believe there was no alternative to your travelling so far alone."

Ilouka did not answer because she felt that if she did so, the argument would go on forever.

"I would like to go up to my room now, Aunt Agatha," she said, "to wash my hands and face. The last part of the journey was very dusty."

"It is not surprising, for we are sadly in need of rain," Mrs. Adolphus replied. "Goodness knows what will happen to the crops if we do not have a shower soon."

Ilouka turned towards the door and as she reached it Mrs. Adolphus said, almost as if she hated to give her good news:

"By the way, Ilouka, you will find a letter from your

mother lying in the Hall. I recognised the handwriting.
I expect she is missing you."

"A letter from Mama? How wonderful!"

Ilouka did not wait to hear any more but went out
into the Hall and saw, carefully placed on one side of
the table where it would not be obvious when she
arrived, a letter addressed in her mother's handwriting.

She picked it up and ran up the stairs where she
could be alone to read it in the plain, rather austere
room that she had occupied the last time she had stayed
at Stone House.

She went to the window, feeling that although it was
still quite light, the gloom inside the house made it
difficult to see clearly.

Then as she opened her mother's letter the very first
words danced before her eyes.

She read:

*I have good news for you, my darling. Lord Denton
has proposed to Muriel and she has accepted him. The
engagement will be in the "Gazette" tomorrow morning.*

*What I know will make you happy is that His
Lordship's Mother is living in France for the good of
her health, and Muriel is going there with his sister as a
Chaperone, so that she can become acquainted with her
future Mother-in-Law.*

*Lord Denton is insistent that they should stay with
his Mother for at least a month, which means you can
come home immediately, and I will present you to the
King and Queen before Muriel returns.*

*I have discussed the matter of Muriel's presentation
with Lord Denton, who is a charming young man, and
he thinks that his Mother would wish to present Muriel
on her marriage, so that makes everything much easier
for you and me.*

*I am afraid your Step-Father is unlikely to send his
horses so far as Stone House, even though I think in his
heart he will be very glad to see you back.*

Will you and Hannah therefore take the Stage-Coach

as far as St. Albans, and I have persuaded your step-father to send our horses to await you there at The Peacock Inn.

You will get this letter on Wednesday and they will be waiting for you on Friday, which will give you time to make yourself pleasant to Mrs. Adolphus, as she might not like you to leave immediately you arrive.

Ilouka gave a little exclamation of delight before she read any more.

Because today was in fact Thursday, this meant she could leave first thing tomrrow morning.

"Thank goodness!" she said to herself. "I can go home and not stay here more than one night!"

It was such a lovely thought that for a moment, although the sky was overcast, the sun seemed to be shining.

While she was reading the letter her trunks had been brought upstairs and an elderly, rather disagreeable housemaid was regarding them balefully.

"You need not unpack them, Josephine," Ilouka said. "I am leaving tomorrow. My mother needs me at home."

She did not wait for the maid to answer, but throwing her bonnet down on the nearest chair she ran down the stairs to tell Aunt Agatha the news, already anticipating how annoyed she would be at having to send somebody with her as far as St. Albans.

She could not be allowed to travel there alone, after Mrs. Adolphus had made so much fuss about it already.

'I am going home! Home!' Ilouka thought delightedly, and her feet seemed to fly down the stairs.

Then as she walked more sedately across the Hall she found herself thinking of the Earl and wondering if by now he had returned from the races to find that she was no longer there.

'What will he do?' she wondered.

Without meaning to, she stood still.

She could almost feel his fingers under her chin, turning her face up to his.

She could see the smile on his lips which was different from any smile she had noticed before.

She felt again the strange sensation his lips had given her pulsating through her body, her vibrations reaching out towards him.

He was carrying her to the top of the snow-capped mountains to the music of a thousand gypsy violins.

Chapter Six

Because the sun was shining as she looked out over the London Street, Ilouka kept thinking of the glinting gold on the lake at Lavenham.

She did not see the traffic moving past, the horses drawing a smart Phaeton or a closed Brougham, but instead the swans, black and white, moving serenely over the silver water, which made her think of the music to which she had danced.

Ever since she had left the Earl's house when he was away at the races, she had found it impossible not to think of him a thousand times a day, and at night she would lie awake reliving the rapture of his kiss.

At the same time, she told herself that he had forgotten her very existence and the quicker she forgot him the better.

But somehow he was always with her, in a shaft of sunlight, in a Hurdy-Gurdy playing a sentimental song in the street.

An errand-boy whistling *Bring My Broom* would bring him back to her so vividly that she felt she must cry out with the pain of it.

"How can I have been so ridiculous as to fall in love with a man who only wanted to make me his mistress and would doubtless have become bored with me very quickly?" she admonished herself.

Yet she knew there was something between her and

the Earl that was timeless and part of eternity, and however long she lived and however many men she knew, she would never be able to forget him.

Because her mother was so elated at the idea that she could take her to London for the Season and present her to King William and Queen Adelaide without Muriel, Ilouka tried for her sake to enter into the excitement of it.

However, she knew that all the time her heart was aching, and although she told herself it was absurd, the ache continued.

'It is just because I had met so few men,' she thought, 'that the Earl seemed to me so impressive, so handsome, and so irresistible.'

She was aware now that her initial feeling of resentment against him was merely because from the very first moment she heard about him, and certainly when she saw him, he seemed different.

Lady Armstrong had been horrified at hearing of Hannah's death.

But she accepted without asking too many uncomfortable questions that after Ilouka had stayed at the Vicarage and attended Hannah's Funeral she had hired a Post-Chaise to take her to Bedfordshire.

"That was very sensible of you, dearest," she said, "although perhaps unconventional."

"There was nothing else I could do, Mama. Aunt Agatha of course was shocked, but quite frankly, I could not face a Stage-Coach again after what had...happened."

"Of course not," her mother agreed, "and you did the only thing possible in the circumstances. I am only thankful that you had enough money."

"Only just enough, Mama I have come home penniless!"

"That is easily remedied," her mother answered. "Your step-father has been very generous over your Season in London and he has not only given me a large sum of money for your clothes and mine, but also promised that you shall have your Ball before Muriel returns from France."

"Oh, Mama, that is wonderful!" Ilouka replied.

She had to force the enthusiasm into her voice, for the mere idea of dancing brought back only too vividly how she had danced in the Earl's Dining-Room.

They had set off for London two days after Ilouka's return home.

The preoccupations of packing, finding a lady's-maid to replace Hannah, and opening Sir James's house in London made it easier to think of other things rather than the Earl.

But at night there were no distractions, and Ilouka would find herself recapturing the rapture and ecstasy she had felt when his kiss had lifted her up to the snowy peaks of the mountains and the world was left behind.

"I had no idea that love was like this," she told herself over and over again.

If she was a little quieter than usual and sometimes there were dark shadows under her eyes in the morning, Lady Armstrong did not appear to notice.

She was so ambitious that her daughter should be acclaimed for her beauty that she was concentrating on supplying her with gowns that would accentuate her white skin and bring out the red lights in her shining hair.

There was no doubt of Ilouka's success from the moment they attended their first dinner-party.

It was given by the Duchess of Bolton, who was an old friend of Sir James Armstrong, and when Ilouka entered the Drawing-Room, in which a large number of people were already assembled, there was a hush.

Ilouka did not realise that her appearance was so sensational, but Lady Armstrong did and she was very proud.

After that the invitations poured in and Lady Armstrong said to her husband with a smile:

"I do not think we shall have Ilouka on our hands for very long. She has already had four proposals of marriage, and I can see the words trembling on the lips of two very eligible young Peers."

"There is no hurry for her to make up her mind," Sir James replied. "At the same time, my darling, I cannot pretend that I would not like to have you to myself."

"You are very kind," Lady Armstrong answered, "and you know I am grateful."

"What I want is that you should be happy."

Lady Armstrong lifted his hand to her cheek with a gesture that he found very touching.

"I am happy," she said, "and sometimes I can hardly believe it when after I became a widow I was so desperately miserable."

"I will never allow you to be that again," Sir James said and kissed her.

"I ought to be the happiest girl in London," Ilouka told herself.

Yet she felt guilty because she knew that despite her resolution to forget the Earl she found herself looking for him at every Ball she attended, at every dinner-party, and searching for a glimpse of his Phaeton when they drove in the Park.

"Forget him! Forget him! Forget him!" she said to herself over and over again.

But still she could feel his fingers under her chin, turning her face up to his, and feel the strength of his arms holding her close against him.

"Tomorrow we are going to the 'Drawing-Room,'" Lady Armstrong said one evening. "I hope, darling child, you will enjoy it as much as I shall. It is eleven years since I was last at Buckingham Palace."

"I expect it still looks very much the same," Ilouka replied.

"It had only just been altered by King George IV and was a sensation!" Lady Armstrong went on. "It certainly seemed to me to be very impressive, but I was very shy in those days, which is more than you have ever been, my dearest."

"I have not been shy," Ilouka replied, "because you and Papa always treated me not as a child whom you talked down to as an inferior but almost as if I were grown-up. That prevented me from being shy and also sharpened my brain."

"It seems almost too much that you should be clever as well as beautiful!" her mother said. "And any man you marry will appreciate that you are not just a pretty face with which he will quickly grow bored."

Ilouka did not reply, but she was thinking that the Earl had appreciated only her face, and they had not been acquainted long enough for him to find her intelligent.

The next evening when she was dressed in the new gown which Lady Armstrong had bought for her presentation, she had to admit that she looked sensational.

Because plain white was not really a colour that complemented the magnolia-like quality of her skin, Lady Armstrong had chosen a gown that was predominately silver.

It had silver ribbons, and the pure silk of which it was made was embroidered all over with a silver design picked out in diamanté.

It had a full skirt, a tiny waist, and was very much a young girl's gown.

At the same time, it was so imaginative that it instantly made Ilouka remember that Mr. Archer had described her in his introduction as "a nymph rising from the lake."

The silver of her gown made her think of the lake at Lavenham, and her step-father gave her as a present a small collet of diamonds to wear round her throat, which glittered with every movement she made.

"You look lovely!" he answered. "Really you need very little ornamentation."

It was a compliment which she knew was sincere, and it illustrated how lucky her mother and she were to have somebody so kind to look after them.

'Mama does not love him in the same way that she loved Papa,' she thought to herself, 'but she does love him, although in a different way, and perhaps I could

feel the same about some other man and therefore feel
I could marry him.'

She knew if she was honest that what she wanted was
the same love that her father and mother had had for
each other and which she knew in her heart was what
she felt for the Earl.

Last night when she had lain awake thinking of him,
she had wondered what would have happened if, instead of running away, she had stayed on for another
night at Lavenham as he had wished her to do.

When he had kissed her it had been so wonderful
that she could still feel herself tremble as she thought of
his lips touching hers.

It suddenly struck her that he might have to come to
her bedroom for another reason other than to save her
from Lord Marlowe.

It now occurred to Ilouka that she had been very
stupid and obtuse.

She had taken it for granted that the Earl had come
to her through the communicating door because he had
heard the noise Lord Marlowe was making outside in
the passage.

It was only now for the first time that she remembered
that when she had turned round and begged him to
save her, he had looked astonished at the furniture she
was staking against the door and seemed for a moment
not to realise why she was doing it.

Then he had gone away to deal with Lord Marlowe.

If he had come to her room without realising what
was happening, what was the point of his visit?

Because Ilouka was so innocent and inexperienced,
and because the Earl seemed so aloof and in her own
words "omnipotent," it had never crossed her mind
that the reason why her room had been changed and
that he had come to her wearing a robe and obviously
undressed was that he had intended to make love to
her.

What that entailed she had no idea, but she knew it

was something wrong and very improper when a man and woman were not married.

It could occur, she thought, between gentlemen and actresses like Madame Vestris, but it was something that was too immodest and wicked to be suggested to a Lady.

"He believed me to be an actress, and that was why he assumed I would agree to something so outrageous," Ilouka told herself.

Suddenly she was extremely unhappy not only because she had lost the Earl but also because she realised that he did not think of her as a Lady to respect and admire, but as an actress whom he could treat insultingly in the same way as Lord Marlowe had insulted her.

It was a revelation which hurt even more than she was hurt already.

Then she knew she had no-one to blame but herself for having agreed in the first place to Mr. Archer's proposition to go with him to entertain the Earl and his friends.

Because she now recognised what she was sure was the truth of the whole situation, she could only pray even more fervently than she was doing already that her mother would never discover what had happened.

'Mama would not only be horrified,' Ilouka thought, 'she would be deeply hurt and upset that I should behave so badly.'

"You look really beautiful, Miss!" the maid who helped her to dress exclaimed when Ilouka took a last look at herself in the mirror before she went downstairs.

"Thank you," she answered.

The three ostrich-feathers at the back of her head were very becoming.

It was at the Battle of Crecy in 1346 that the Black Prince won both his spurs and the famous ostrich-plumes which adorned his seals as Prince of Wales.

Young girls when they were presented to the Monarch had worn them ever since then.

"There won't be anyone as beautiful as you are at the Ball, Miss, I'm certain of that!" the maid went on.

Ilouka smiled her thanks, but she was thinking that there was one person who would never admire her except for her looks, but whom she wanted above all things to admire her character, her personality, and her mind.

"Forget him! Forget him! Forget him!" her feet seemed to say as she went lightly down the stairs.

As they drove to Buckingham Palace in Sir James's smart London carriage, she thought the wheels were repeating the same words.

Lady Armstrong looked lovely in a gown of pale mauve and wearing a tiara of amethysts and diamonds with a necklace of the same stones.

She carried a bouquet of mauve orchids which Sir James had given her, while for Ilouka there was a little posy of white roses that were just coming into bloom.

It made her think of the roses she had worn on top of her head and round her wrists when she had danced at Lavenham.

"You look like Persephone going down into Hades," Mr. Archer had told her.

Because of what had happened, she thought she would never be able to escape from the darkness but must remain there and never again find spring in her heart.

Then because she told herself she was being extremely ungrateful, she smiled at her step-father sitting opposite her and looking extremely smart in his uniform as Deputy Lord Lieutenant of Buckinghamshire.

"I know one thing," he said to his wife, "no man in the Palace will be able to present two such beautiful women as I am doing!"

"You cannot say that until you have had a look round," Lady Armstrong teased, "and Ilouka and I will be very apprehensive in case, dearest James, we are eclipsed by one of the beautiful women whom you knew before you married me."

"Since I married you," Sir James replied, "I have never been able to notice any other woman."

Ilouka was not listening but was thinking that the actress from Drury Lane in whom the Earl was interested must certainly be not only more beautiful than she was but much more talented.

"He will watch her performance night after night," she told herself, "and will soon forget the very amateur way in which I danced for him in his Dining-Room."

There was a little wait as they reached the courtyard of Buckingham Palace, where there were at least a dozen carriages ahead of them.

Then gradually, as the occupants were set down to enter the Palace, they drew nearer and eventually a powdered footman opened the door and Lady Armstrong stepped out.

Ilouka followed her and after they had deposited their wraps they went up a wide staircase covered in red carpet towards the Throne-Room, where the King and Queen were holding court.

It took some time to move up the stairs where the Gentlemen-at-Arms were on guard, and Ilouka thought it would be interesting to see Queen Adelaide, who had married King William in 1818 although he was very much older than she was.

People were always talking about her at her mother's parties, and while some spoke of her as "an amiable little woman," others, more critical, described her as "small, mouse-like, and excessively dull."

There were always those who were ready to gossip about the Royal Family, and Sir James said now in a low voice to his wife:

"I suppose you have heard that the odious Duchess of Kent has refused to allow Princess Victoria to attend any of the Royal Drawing-Rooms?"

"Has she really!" Lady Armstrong exclaimed. "That is too bad, when she knows that the King is so fond of his niece."

They moved on slowly until at last they reached the

Throne-Room. Ilouka could now see that Queen Adelaide, seated at the far end of it and blazing with jewels, did in fact look very small and mouse-like beside her large, stout, ageing husband.

The King was almost bald, and what hair he did have was dead white, but he smiled at everybody who was presented and Ilouka was sure that the stories about his being very kind and unpretentious were true.

A friend of Sir James's came up to speak to them, and Ilouka heard him say:

"These formal affairs bore me stiff! I must admit that things were far more amusing when King George was alive."

Sir James laughed.

"You certainly have to behave yourself better these days, Arthur."

"That is true," his friend replied, "but the evenings at Court are insufferable. The King snoozes, the Queen does needlework, and we are not supposed to discuss politics."

Sir James laughed again, and Ilouka thought that the Earl certainly had more lively evenings than those her step-father's friend described.

Now she could see the presentations taking place and a Lord-in-Waiting was calling out the names:

"The Duchess of Bolton presenting Lady Mary Fotheringay-Stuart! Lady Ashburton presenting the Honourable Jane Trant and Miss Nancy Carrington!"

The Lord-in-Waiting had a somewhat monotonous voice and Ilouka looked round at the gilt and white walls against which the sparkling tiaras of the ladies seemed to glow almost as if they held the sunlight in them.

Then it was her turn and she was in a line where every lady was being careful not to stand on the train of the one in front of her.

The Lord-in-Waiting was intoning their names almost as if they were in Church.

"The Countess Hull, presenting Lady Penelope Curtis!"

Then in exactly the same tone:

"Lady Armstrong, presenting Miss Ilouka Compton!

Her mother moved forward ahead of Ilouka to sink down in a low curtsey in front of the Queen, who inclined her head, and then Lady Armstrong moved on to curtsey to the King.

Ilouka took her place.

As she curtseyed very carefully, her back straight, holding her head high, the Queen smiled at her, and she instinctively smiled back.

Then as her mother walked away she moved on to the King.

She made an even lower curtsey than she had to the Queen, and as she rose she heard the King say in his blunt manner:

"Pretty girl! Very pretty!"

His comments were known to be often disconcerting, but because it was a compliment Ilouka could not help smiling at him, thinking that he was speaking to himself.

Then distinctly she heard a voice say:

"I agree with you, Sire."

She raised her eyes and her heart seemed to turn over in her breast.

At the same time she felt unable to move, for standing behind the King's chair, resplendent in glittering decorations, the blue ribbon of the Order of the Garter across his chest, was the Earl.

Ilouka met his eyes, until with what was an almost superhuman effort she rose from her curtsey and moved away to follow her mother.

For a moment she could not think, and was aware only that her whole body was pulsating with the fact that she had seen the Earl again and, what was more, that he must have recognised her.

She wondered frantically what he would think or what he would say now that he knew who she really was.

She was so bemused with the shock of seeing him in such circumstances that it was impossible to think, let alone speak.

Sir James had joined them and was introducing her mother to his friends. They spoke to Ilouka, and she supposed that she answered them coherently.

At the same time, she felt as if she were in another world, having stepped into a "No-Man's-Land" where it was impossible for her to feel that anything was real but the beating of her heart.

She must have talked to dozens of people in the next hour, accepted compliments and apparently answered the questions they asked her with some degree of sense.

It was only when the King, leading the Queen by the hand, had left the Throne-Room and passed through the midst of their guests to speak occasionally to someone in particular before they finally disappeared, that it was possible for anybody to leave.

"Can we go now, Mama?" Ilouka asked.

"There is no hurry, darling," Lady Armstrong replied. "I am enjoying myself, and your step-father is anxious to find a particular friend to whom he wishes to introduce me."

Ilouka could not tell her mother that she wished to leave before she was forced to encounter the Earl.

She looked apprehensively about her at the people gossiping, expecting him to approach her at any moment with an accusing look in his eyes.

Then unexpectedly when she was looking in another direction she heard his voice say:

"Good-evening, Armstrong! I did not expect to see you here!"

"Hello, Lavenham!" Sir James replied. "That is what I should say to you. I thought you would be too busy with your horses to have time for such formalities as this."

"I was pressured into doing my duty," the Earl replied.

"I do not think you have met my wife," Sir James said with a smile. "Dearest, let me present the Earl of Lavenham, who, as you are aware, has the finest stable in the country and wins all the Classic races so that none of the rest of us ever get a look-in."

Lady Armstrong held out her hand.

"I have heard of you for years, My Lord," she said, "and I am so pleased to meet you in person."

"You are very kind."

The Earl's eyes turned towards Ilouka and Sir James said:

"Now you will meet the reason for my appearance here today. My wife and I wished to present my step-daughter to their Majesties."

The Earl bowed as Ilouka curtseyed, and because she found it impossible to look at him, her eye-lashes were dark against her cheeks.

"I am delighted to make your acquaintance, Miss Compton," he said.

Ilouka was sure there was a sarcastic note in his voice, but because she thought it would seem strange if she said nothing, she forced herself to reply:

"I have... heard of your... magnificent horses... My Lord."

"I hope one day to show them to you," he said, "when you can spare the time to visit my stables."

Ilouka drew in her breath.

She knew he was reproaching her for having left before she could see Apollo and his other horses.

He was looking at her and she wondered if he was regarding her with contempt.

Then she was suddenly afraid, desperately afraid that he would say something which would reveal to her mother that they had met before and the whole story of her deception would have to be unfolded.

Because she was so apprehensive, it was impossible for her to judge the expression in the Earl's grey eyes.

Instead, she could only feel her vibrations pulsating towards him and was afraid that what she was feeling would be obvious not only to him but also to her mother and her step-father.

Then, coming to deliver her at the eleventh hour

from a predicament which she felt totally unable to cope with, a lilting voice exclaimed:

"James! How wonderful to see you! And why have you been neglecting me for so long?"

A woman glittering with sapphires, and wearing a blue gown that echoed the blue of her eyes, moved between the Earl and Sir James and slipped her arm through his.

For a moment the newcomer isolated Ilouka and the Earl from her mother and step-father, and when he would have started to speak, Ilouka said unhappily:

"I . . . I . . . must . . . explain."

"I have to see you," the Earl said, "and as you say, you have a lot of explaining to do."

"I . . . know."

"Where can I meet you alone?"

She tried to think coherently of some place where they could talk without being overheard.

As if the Earl understood her difficulty, he said:

"I shall be riding in the Park early tomorrow morning and will be at the Achilles statue at seven o'clock."

Ilouka had only just heard the words before her mother was at her side, saying:

"I want you, dearest, to meet the French Ambassador and his wife."

"Yes, of course, Mama."

"And I must return to my duties," the Earl remarked. "Good-night, Lady Armstrong. Good-night, Miss Compton."

He bowed somewhat formally and moved away towards a group of foreign Royalty and Ambassadors who were obviously waiting to be entertained by the senior members of the Royal Household.

As Ilouka watched him go she felt as if he was walking out of her life as she had walked out of his.

Then she told herself with a sudden leap of her heart that at least she would see him tomorrow.

It would be embarrassing to have to tell him why she had pretended to be an actress, and he would doubtless

be angry and reproachful. At the same time, she would
see him and that was all that mattered.

She could never remember exactly what happened
for the rest of the evening.

As they were driven home her mother was talking
excitedly about the grandeur of the Palace, while Sir
James was, Ilouka thought, a little apologetic about the
effusive manner in which he had been greeted by a lady
who was quite obviously an "old flame."

But their voices seemed far away and nothing she
heard appeared to make sense.

Only as they reached the house did Ilouka realise
that she had somehow to ride in the Park the following
morning without either her mother or Sir James being
aware of what she was doing.

If she said she was riding, undoubtedly Sir James
would accompany her, or her mother might think it
best for her to rest in the morning, as she had done
since she had been in London, because there would be
another Ball in the evening.

'I have to see him!' Ilouka thought to herself, but she
could not imagine how it could be managed.

In the end, after they had had a late supper, she went
up to bed, still thinking of how she could leave the
house without anybody being aware of it.

It was impossible to sleep, and a dozen times during
the night she rose to go to the window to look up at the
star-lit sky, wondering what the Earl was thinking about
her.

She was certain that he would be angry and inevitably shocked by her behaviour.

But what was really important was to make him
promise not to reveal to her mother or Sir James the
reprehensible way she had behaved.

It was the longest night Ilouka had ever spent.

When as she stood at the window she heard in the far
distance a clock strike the hour of five, she thought a
century had passed since she had seen the Earl and had

known as he walked away from her that she was no longer of any importance to him.

The position he had offered her in his life was that of a woman whose only asset as far as he was concerned was that she had a pretty face.

It was an humiliation that Ilouka had somehow never expected would happen to her.

She had been brought up to believe that it was personality that counted more than looks, and while she was deeply grateful that people thought her beautiful, she knew that she had something more to offer them.

This was intrinsically *herself*, and therefore very valuable as far as she was concerned.

But as a dancer, an actress, a woman who could become a man's mistress, she was a dispensable possession who counted far less than a race-horse.

'That is what he feels for me,' she thought.

She felt at that moment that she was in a deep, dark hell from which she would never be able to escape.

Then as gradually the first rays of the sun appeared over the roof-tops and the sky lightened, she knew the night had passed and she would be able to see the Earl.

But she knew bitterly that while she would see him and be near him, she would have to humble herself and apologise for a deception which he would condemn utterly as an outrageous action by a woman who he now knew had been born a Lady.

She thought perhaps it would be wiser not to go to him where he would be waiting for her at the Achilles statue.

Then she knew that if she did not go, he might come to the house and tell her mother that they had met in very different circumstances.

Suddenly she decided what she would do and quickly dressed herself in her riding-habit.

Sir James's horses were stabled behind the house and could be reached from a back door which opened onto the Mews.

Because they were out every night, Lady Armstrong

would not be called before nine o'clock, and because Sir James always breakfasted downstairs at eight-thirty, Ilouka knew if she left at half-past-six she would be safe from being seen.

She dressed herself with care, arranging her hair in a neat chignon beneath a riding-hat with a high crown which was encircled by a gauze veil.

Riding-habits had become very much fuller in the skirts in the last year or so. They had small waists and neat little jackets over white muslin blouses which fastened with a bow at the neck.

Her habit made Ilouka look very young, and yet beneath the severity of her hat her hair glowed like the flames from a gypsy fire.

Her eyes too seemed to fill her small face because she was apprehensive.

Having ordered a horse to be saddled, she rode out of the Mews towards the Park, accompanied by a sleepy groom who was resenting being called out on duty so early in the morning.

He rode several paces behind her, and because Ilouka knew she had to kill time before the Earl would be at the Achilles statue at seven o'clock, she went not towards Hyde Park Corner but the other way round the Park.

She crossed the Serpentine by the bridge, galloping her horse over the unfashionable grass where there was nobody to see her except a few small boys kicking a ball about.

Then she rode slowly down Rotten Row, which was also empty save for some athletic young gentlemen who preferred to ride before there was any sign of the fashionable ladies in their carriages who would require them to stop and chatter.

It was only as the statue of Achilles appeared ahead of her that Ilouka felt her heart beating convulsively.

Then she saw the Earl seated astride a huge black stallion and she had a sudden longing to turn her horse round and gallop away.

But it was too late. He had seen her, and as if he drew her like a magnet she rode slowly towards him, feeling as if she were being carried to the guillotine.

She drew in her horse and stared at him, her eyes very wide and, although she did not realise it, frightened.

The Earl swept his hat from his head.

"Good-morning, Miss Compton!"

"Good-morning... My... Lord."

There was a little tremor in her voice that she could not repress, and she thought there was a cynical twist to his lips before he said:

"Shall we ride towards the Serpentine?"

"Yes... that would... be very... pleasant."

She thought her voice seemed to come in a strange jerk, and yet it was impossible to control it.

They turned their horses and walked side by side, her groom keeping well behind them.

Because Ilouka felt it was impossible to speak, there was silence and the Earl seemed to have no inclination to talk.

They rode until they reached the Serpentine, which was glittering gold in the morning sun.

The Earl reined in his horse.

"I think it would be a good idea," he said, "if we left our horses with your groom and walked a little way in the trees to find a seat where we can talk."

"Yes... of course... if that is what you... want," Ilouka replied.

The Earl beckoned the groom forward as he dismounted and handed him the reins of his stallion, giving him an order in a voice that sounded to Ilouka a little sharp, as if he was in a bad temper.

Then he came to the side of her horse and lifted her down.

As he put his hands on her small waist and she was close to him, she felt a sensation like a streak of lightning flash through her and she knew that however angry he might be, she loved him.

If only he would kiss her once more, she thought,

that would be the most wonderful thing that could happen.

Then she was free and the Earl gave the reins of her horse to the groom.

Slowly she walked ahead along a little path which led them towards a profusion of bushes underneath the birch trees.

Almost before she expected it she came upon a seat that was set back amongst some shrubs. This seemed the obvious place and she sat down.

As she did so she realised that it would be impossible for anybody to see them unless they were boating on the Serpentine.

Because she was nervous she arranged her skirts very carefully, aware for the moment that the Earl had not sat beside her but was looking down at her from his great height.

He might, she thought wryly, be on the pedestal she had imagined him to be occupying when she had seen him sitting at the end of the dining-table and knew that he would never step down from it to mix with the common herd.

Then he seated himself beside her, and turning sideways as he had done when they sat on the sofa in the *Boudoir* together at Lavenham, he put his arm along the back of the seat.

At the same time he lifted his tall-hat and set it down on the ground beside him.

Then with what she thought was a grim note in his voice he said:

"Well, Miss Ilouka Ganymede, what have you to say for yourself?"

Ilouka drew in her breath.

"I . . . I am sorry," she said. "I did not . . . mean to do anything wrong . . . but I know now that it was in fact very . . . very wrong of me to . . . come to your . . . house."

"It was not only very wrong, it was crazy!" the Earl

replied. "How could you pretend to be understudying Madame Vestris, and . . ."

He stopped. Then he said:

"Never mind *what* you did. I want to know *why*!"

"If I . . . tell you the whole . . . truth," Ilouka said in a very small voice, "will you . . . promise, will you swear by . . . everything you hold sacred . . . that you will not tell Mama?"

"I suppose to tell her is what I ought to do," the Earl answered.

Ilouka gave a little cry.

"Please . . . please . . . I beg of you . . . if you tell her she will not only be angry with me . . . but very . . . very hurt that I should behave in such a reprehensible manner."

"I am not surprised," the Earl said grimly.

"I did not . . . expect to see . . . you at the Palace," Ilouka said impulsively. "I had thought . . . if I saw you elsewhere . . . I would be able to . . . ask you before you . . . met Mama not to . . . reveal to her my . . . indiscretion . . ."

"So that is what you call it," the Earl said. "I can think of a far more positive description of your behaviour."

"I know," Ilouka said unhappily, "but it just . . . happened that I became . . . involved, and I did not . . . realise what might . . . happen."

"I suppose you were unaware of the dangers you ran."

Ilouka thought of Lord Marlowe and shuddered.

"But you . . . saved me."

There was a little pause. Then the Earl remarked in a dry voice she knew so well:

"Yes, I saved you from Lord Marlowe—but not from myself!"

He watched the colour flood into her cheeks before she said in a low voice:

"I never . . . thought for a moment that . . . sort of thing would . . . h-happen. I was just trying to . . . help Mr. Archer."

"Did you not realise that when you pretended to be the understudy to Madame Vestris there would be men approaching you as Marlowe tried to do?"

"I swear to you it . . . never entered . . . my head. I had of course heard of . . . Madame Vestris . . . and I knew that . . . Mama thought her . . . improper because she wore breeches on the stage . . . but I had not thought of her in any other way until after . . ."

She stopped, as if she had no words, and the Earl finished quietly:

". . . I offered you my protection. I presume you understand what that means?"

"I do . . . now," Ilouka said in a low voice, "but only because Mr. Archer said that Miss Ganymede . . . whose place I had taken, had lost her . . . Protector, which was . . . why she wanted the money that you were . . . prepared to pay for the . . . entertainment."

"What happened to Miss Ganymede?"

Ilouka drew in her breath.

"She and my lady's-maid, Hannah . . . were killed when the Stage-Coach in which we were travelling turned over."

The way she spoke was very revealing, and as she looked up at him she saw that the Earl was staring at her incredulously.

"The Stage-Coach in which you were travelling turned over?" he repeated, as if he thought he could not have heard correctly what she said.

"Yes, my step-father did not wish to send me in a carriage because it was too tiring for the horses, so H-Hannah and I were . . . going in the Stage-Coach to Bedfordshire."

"Why were you going there?"

"Because my . . . step-father's daughter . . . Muriel, hates me . . . and Lord Denton, whom she hoped would marry her . . . was coming . . ."

Ilouka suddenly threw up her hands and said:

"Oh . . . it is all so complicated . . . and such a long story . . . and if I tell you . . . you will never believe it!"

"I am trying to believe it," the Earl said, "but it is certainly somewhat involved."

"Of course it is involved," Ilouka retorted. "You do not suppose for a moment that I would have deliberately... impersonated an actress or come to your... house if I had not been put in the... position where it seemed... cruel and heartless to... refuse?"

She spoke passionately. Then she said in a different tone:

"Please... please... try to understand... and do not be angry with me."

"Why should it worry you if I am?" the Earl asked.

There was silence for a moment. Then Ilouka said:

"I am afraid of your being... angry with me and I am... afraid too that you might... tell Mama."

"I will not tell your mother," the Earl answered, "if you promise me that never, never again will you do anything so reprehensible. But I am still interested to know why you should be afraid of my anger."

Ilouka knew she could tell him exactly why she was afraid, and that she wanted him not to be contemptuous and ashamed of her but to admire and respect her.

Then she thought the real truth was none of these things: she wanted him to love her!

She wanted him to kiss her as he had done before, and if that was impossible, then what did it matter what he thought?

She looked away from him, her small straight nose silhouetted against the shrubs as she said:

"You have... obviously made up your mind... about me... and there is no... real point in my... telling you any m-more."

"That may or may not be true," the Earl said. "At the same time, I am interested in your reasons for behaving as you did."

Ilouka did not speak and he went on:

"You came to my house to give a performance which was different in every way from anything I have ever seen before, and as a result you incited one of my guests to behave in a very reprehensible manner!"

His words stung Ilouka and she said angrily:

"That is unfair! Lord Marlowe is a horrible man who had drunk . . . too much, and you cannot blame . . . me because he came knocking on my door. I never . . . dreamt that any gentleman would . . . behave in such a way."

"No gentleman would . . . towards a Lady."

"I thought of that," Ilouka said, "and as I know you do not think I am a Lady, and as you . . . despise me . . . there is no point in our going on talking. I can only say that I am . . . ashamed of myself . . . and yet I know I would have felt guilty for the rest of my life if I had . . . refused to help Mr. Archer when it was his . . . last chance."

"That is the story which I am waiting to hear," the Earl said quietly.

"W-why should you be . . . interested?" Ilouka asked.

Her voice trembled a little because she felt he was making it difficult for her, and also because it was all too impossible to explain.

Then as she spoke she turned to look at him.

Her eyes met his and her anger ebbed away.

She could only see his grey eyes and feel as if they filled the whole world.

Chapter Seven

"That is what happened," Ilouka said. "I promise you it is the truth, and there seemed to be nothing else I could do."

She had told the Earl exactly what happened from the moment her step-father had said Lord Denton was coming to stay and Muriel had insisted that she was not to be at The Towers when he was there.

She felt that the Earl looked a little sympathetic as she explained how jealous Muriel was of her.

When she went on to describe how after the Stage-Coach had turned over Hannah and Lucille Ganymede had been crushed to death, she thought his eyes hardened, and there was a tight line to his lips.

Because she was nervous she faltered and stumbled over the part where she had not only wanted to help Mr. Archer but had also felt it would be a relief not to hurry on to Bedfordshire.

She knew that in a way she was condemning herself by being so honest, but at the same time something compelled her to tell the Earl the truth, whatever he might think of her.

"It was so exciting to see your . . . wonderful house," she said, "and because it was an . . . adventure which Papa would have . . . enjoyed, I did not feel as . . . guilty as I suppose I ought to have done."

"It did not strike you that you should have a Chaperone when staying in a house where all the guests were men?" the Earl asked.

The colour came into Ilouka's face and she said a little incoherently:

"Of course I . . . knew I would have . . . needed a Chaperone if I had been staying there as . . . myself, but I did not . . . think Miss Ganymede would have . . . required one."

"And you did not wonder why there was no need for her to be chaperoned?"

"No . . . not until after Lord Marlowe . . . tried to . . . get into . . . my bedroom."

"The only excuse I can find for your behaviour is that you are very young and inexperienced," the Earl said as if he spoke to himself.

"And very . . . foolish," Ilouka added miserably.

She sighed and the Earl said:

"What do you expect me to do now?"

"All I am asking is that you . . . promise not to tell Mama . . . or my step-father."

"I will not do that," he said. "At the same time, you are aware I was not the only person present at my dinner-party."

Ilouka looked at him with wide eyes. Then she said:

"I had . . . forgotten that your . . . guests might . . . know my step-father, as you . . . do."

He did not speak and she said frantically:

"Surely they will not . . . connect me as a . . . débutante with . . . somebody who danced and sang for them once as . . . an entertainer?"

"You are not a person one forgets easily," the Earl replied, "and without flattering you, I must say that your dance was unusual. Inevitably, anybody who saw it will talk about it, especially as it took place in my house."

Almost as if he conjured up a picture, Ilouka could hear the gentlemen who had sat round the table with its gold and silver ornaments telling their friends at the Club what sort of entertainment the Earl of Lavenham had provided for them after they had been racing all day.

She clasped her fingers together and asked:

"What . . . shall I do? What . . . can I do?"

"I think for the moment," the Earl replied, "we must just hope that the gentlemen present, who were mostly older men devoted to racing, will not be present at the Balls to which you have been invited."

Ilouka gave a deep sigh.

"Why did I not . . . think of this . . . before?"

"Unfortunately, none of us can turn back the clock," the Earl said drily, "and because you cannot risk being talked about again, I think the best thing you can do at this moment is to continue your ride, then try to forget what happened before you started your Season in London."

"And will you . . . forget that you ever . . . met me before last . . . night?" she asked.

"Shall I say I will not speak of it," he answered.

"But supposing one of your friends asks you how he can meet Miss Ganymede?"

The Earl's lips twisted a little mockingly.

"I shall refer him to Madame Vestris, who will doubtless be aware by now of what has happneed to her understudy."

Ilouka was silent before she said:

"Thank you for not being so . . . angry with me now as I . . . think you were . . . last night."

"I was astonished to see you," the Earl replied. "I never imagined I would meet at Buckingham Palace the dancer and singer I employed to amuse my guests."

"It does sound . . . strange when you put it like . . . that," Ilouka said unhappily.

"And shall I add that I was delighted that my search for you was ended."

For the moment Ilouka was still. Then she turned to look at him.

"You were . . . searching for me?" she asked incredulously.

"I was extremely perturbed as to what had happened. I could hardly believe that you would sneak away without saying good-bye and without telling me where you were going."

"How could I do.... anything else?"

"In the circumstances, I suppose it was a sensible thing to do!" the Earl answered. "But at the time I could not imagine what reason you had for leaving in such a reprehensible manner."

She knew as he spoke that he was thinking that any woman to whom he offered his protection would be only too willing to accept it.

It flashed through her mind that it was strange that he should have wanted her when he already had the actress who played at Drury Lane to amuse him.

Then she knew it was a question she could not ask, and said:

"I suppose I was being very... foolish in thinking I would... never see you... again."

"It obviously did not perturb you," the Earl replied, "while I was afraid you might be in trouble of some sort."

"You... wanted to... help me?"

"I was willing to do so."

"That was kind of you, but you know now that I do not need your help."

"I am well aware that your step-father is a rich man," the Earl said drily.

As he spoke, Ilouka thought she did not need help from him, but something very different; something he must never know or realise.

She wondered what he would think if she asked him to kiss her just once more before, now that he knew who she was and was aware that she was well looked after, she no longer concerned him.

Instead she said in a very small voice:

"I suppose... now I shall... never see Apollo... or your other horses."

The Earl was silent and she wondered if she had been too forward in deliberately asking for an invitation.

Then he said:

"It might be possible when I return to the country, but perhaps because our previous association was rather different, I should ask your mother and step-father and of course you to dine with me one evening."

Because it was a chance of seeing him again, Ilouka felt her heart leap as she said:

"Would you do . . . that?"

"I presume you have an evening free amongst your other engagements?" the Earl remarked.

"Yes, of course."

Ilouka tried to think frantically what they were doing and said:

"Tonight we are dining at Devonshire House."

"I also have been invited," the Earl remarked, "so that will be a good opportunity for me to talk to your step-father and suggest an evening when you can be my guests."

"We shall be free the following night," Ilouka said eagerly, "and I know there is nothing in Mama's diary for next Wednesday."

"I will remember both those dates."

He rose to his feet, saying as he did so:

"It is getting late in the morning and it would be a mistake for you to be talked about. I suggest you ride back through the Row and I will go in the opposite direction."

He spoke so formally that Ilouka felt her heart sink.

She had the frightened feeling that although he had said he would ask her to dinner, when he left her he might change his mind.

Then she remembered she would see him tonight at Devonshire House and that at least would be something to look forward to.

They walked back along the side of the Serpentine in silence.

Then when the horses were just ahead of them the Earl said:

"Enjoy yourself, Ilouka! The Social World can be very entrancing when you are young, before you become bored and disillusioned."

"Is that what you are?"

"I was talking about you," he replied, "and young ladies should not probe too deeply into things that do no concern them."

She thought he was snubbing her and she blushed before she said:

"I am sorry if that was ... something I should not have ... asked, but as you have already pointed out, I do not ... behave as a ... conventional young lady should do."

The Earl gave a short laugh.

"That is certainly true. You are very unpredictable, Ilouka, not only in what you say but in how you look and also in the way you dance."

He stood still, looking at her, before he asked:

"Who taught you how to dance like that?"

"Nobody," Ilouka answered. "It is my Hungarian blood which when I hear gypsy music conjures up pictures which make my feet move as if they can think and feel for themselves."

"What sort of pictures?" the Earl enquired, and it sounded as if he was really interested.

"I see the Hungarian Steppes," Ilouka replied, "and the gypsies in their colourful clothing and their painted caravans. I hear the music of the violins and in the distance see the snow-capped mountains."

She wondered as she spoke a little dreamily what the Earl would say if she told him that when he kissed her it had felt as though he carried her to the top of the mountains and they danced in the snow.

"And your Hungarian blood accounts for the colour of your hair," he said quietly.

"I am like my great-grandmother."

"That explains many things that puzzled me," he said.

But before she could ask him what he meant, he walked towards the horses.

When they reached them he picked her up and lifted her onto the saddle, and as she put her foot in the stirrup the Earl arranged her skirt in an experienced manner.

He then walked to take his stallion from the groom and swing himself into the saddle.

Ilouka watched him, thinking that no man could be more handsome, or, when he was mounted, look finer or more impressive on a horse.

The Earl raised his top-hat.

"Good-day, Miss Compton," he said. "It has been very pleasant meeting you again."

Then without waiting for her reply he trotted off beside the Serpentine.

As she watched him go Ilouka thought that while he had not been as angry as she had expected, it was quite obvious that he was no longer interested in her.

Outrageously, she thought to herself that perhaps she would have been very much happier if she had been under his "protection."

* * *

As they passed through the gold-tipped gates of Devonshire House, Ilouka was aware that her mother was not only delighted at having received the invitation from the Duchess but was also far more excited about the evening ahead of them than she was.

Because all day her thoughts had been only on the Earl, she could not help anticipating that he would pay her little attention at the dinner-party and that she would be left later to dance with the younger men.

Although there had been a number of other girls at the Balls she had attended so far, Ilouka was intelligent enough to realise that the people who enjoyed them most were the older married couples who knew one another intimately.

The ladies too were so elegant and spectacular in their tiaras and fabulous jewels that she could understand that in their simplicity and inexperience the débutantes were not particularly attractive and the gentlemen found older women much more amusing.

She could understand this even better when she talked with the débutantes themselves.

She found that despite the fact that she had always lived in the country and was extremely poor, she was not only better educated but certainly quicker-brained than they were.

She also had a variety of interests that apparently did not appeal to them.

Because her father had always talked of his successes on the Turf, Ilouka knew a great deal about horses.

She suspected that her contemporaries not only knew little about the Classic races but were frightened to ride anything that was not quiet and docile.

They also had no interest in politics, and one girl to whom she talked even confessed that she had no idea who was the Prime Minister and had never heard of the Reform Bill.

'I find them extremely boring,' Ilouka thought scornfully.

Then she wondered if that was what the Earl felt about her.

Apart from the fact of loving him, she knew he was an extremely intelligent man, and because she had searched the newspapers for every mention of his name she found that he frequently spoke in the House of Lords and was an authority on Foreign Affairs.

'If only I could be alone with him for a little while,' she thought wistfully, 'I could make him realise I am not a nit-wit, and there are also so many questions I would like to ask him.'

At the dinner at Devonshire House she looked down

the long table at which she was at the far end and saw
the Earl seated on the left of the Duchess.

He was talking to a very beautiful and heavily bejew-
elled lady on his other side in a way which made Ilouka
suspect there was a special intimacy between them.

'Perhaps that lady is one of his loves,' she thought
unhappily.

Because she was so curious, she asked the gentleman
next to her:

"Do you know who the lady is sitting next to the Earl
of Lavenham?"

He was rather a vacant-looking youth, with a receding
chin, and he replied:

"That is the Marchioness of Doncaster."

"She is very beautiful."

"Lavenham obviously thinks so," her partner replied,
"but then he is noted for having an eye for a horse and
for every pretty woman who comes within his orbit."

He laughed rather spitefully and Ilouka felt as if
there were a heavy stone in her breast which made it
impossible for her to eat any more.

It was with an effort that she turned politely to the
gentleman on the other side of her, who told her a
rather dismal tale of how much he had lost at cards last
week.

He was obviously trying to drown his sorrows by
quickly emptying his glass every time it was refilled.

She tried hard to keep herself from looking at the
Earl and to concentrate on her dinner-partners, but it
was impossible.

When the Marchioness made him laugh it only in-
creased the agony within her to the point where it was
a physical pain.

Finally, and it seemed after a very long time, the
Duchess took the ladies from the Dining-Room, leaving
the gentlemen to their port.

They went upstairs to the bedrooms where Ilouka
tidied her hair. As she did so, she did not see her own

face in the mirror or the very attractive gown she was wearing.

Instead she saw only the seductive eyes of the Marchioness of Doncaster as she looked at the Earl and the provocative movement of her red lips as she talked to him.

"I wish I could go home!" she said, and did not realise she had spoken aloud.

"You must not say that," a girl standing next to her remarked. "Now we can really have fun. There will be dancing and the gardens are lit with fairy-lights and there are little arbours where you can sit with your partner and no-one can see you."

The girl who spoke looked coy, and Ilouka without speaking went to her mother's side.

"Are you enjoying yourself, darling?" Lady Armstrong asked. "I think the dinner was delightful and now the Duchess tells me there are a hundred or more people arriving for the dancing, and I know you will have a wonderful time."

"Yes, of course, Mama," Ilouka answered dutifully.

The music had started in the Ball-Room as they went downstairs.

It was a beautifully proportioned room filled with flowers and had several long windows opening into the garden.

Ilouka saw the fairy-lights edging the borders of the paths and the Chinese lanterns hanging from the branches of the trees.

She thought that a month ago she would have been thrilled to be in such a party.

Now, because she was certain that in a few minutes she would see the Earl dancing with the alluring Marchioness, all she wanted to do was to go away by herself and hide.

When the gentlemen finally began to leave the Dining-Room, she was asked to dance by the young man who had sat next to her at dinner.

As she could not think of a reason for refusing, she

danced with him, but all the time she was watching the door for the Earl.

When he appeared he was talking to the Duke and two other men and Ilouka guessed their conversation was about horses.

That made her feel happier, and she danced more animatedly than she had done before so that her partner paid her compliments and asked her how soon he could dance with her again.

As was correct, she returned to her mother's side and as soon as she reached Lady Armstrong the Duke detached himself from the Earl and came towards her, saying:

"As a very old friend of your husband's, Lady Armstrong, I claim the privilege of dancing with you before he does!"

Lady Armstrong laughed.

"I should be very honoured, Your Grace."

"Then let us show him what we can do," the Duke said.

They moved onto the dance-floor and Ilouka looked round, then suddenly was very still.

Coming through the door with a group of other people who had obviously just arrived she saw something which she knew would be impossible to forget— the red, florid, dissipated face of Lord Marlowe.

She made an inaudible little sound, then slipped out of the room through one of the open windows into the garden.

She ran into the shadows under the trees to stand looking back at the house, hearing the music, and seeing the couples who were dancing past the window.

"What . . . shall I do? What shall . . . I do?" she asked, and knew there was only one person who could answer that question and save her.

She was almost certain that when the Duke had left the Earl to dance with her mother, the Earl had remained where he was talking and was not dancing.

'I must speak to him!' she thought.

Several of the guests were coming from the Ball-Room into the garden and moving amongst them was a footman carrying some satin cushions which he placed along the seats arranged under the trees not far from where Ilouka was standing.

She went up to him.

"Do you know the Earl of Lavenham by sight?" she asked.

"Yes, Miss," the footman replied. "His Lordship's some fine 'orses."

"I think you will find him just inside the door of the Ball-Room," Ilouka said. "Could you draw him aside and tell him I want to speak to him?"

The footman grinned and she knew that he was thinking that the Earl was not only notorious for his horses but also for his love-affairs.

"I'll do that, Miss."

The footman hurried away into the house, entering it by one of the open windows.

There seemed to Ilouka to be a long pause and she was afraid the man could not find the Earl, when suddenly she saw his broad shoulders silhouetted against the light and knew that he was coming to her as she had asked.

She held her breath.

As he reached the top of the steps she saw the footman beside him, indicating to him where she was hiding.

Without hurrying, and walking in a manner which made Ilouka afraid that the Earl thought it was indiscreet for her to have sent for him like this, he crossed the grass to within a few feet of where she stood beside the trunk of a tree.

"Ilouka?" he asked, as if he was not certain she was there.

She came towards him from the shadows.

"I . . . I had to ask you to . . . come here," she said. "I . . . need your help . . . and I need it . . . desperately!"

There was no need for the Earl to see the expression

on her face in the light of the Chinese lanterns, for he could hear the fear in her voice.

"Let us go further away from the house," he said quite calmly, "then you can tell me what is worrying you."

They walked onto the grass, and as the Earl obviously knew the garden, he moved between the trees until they reached a high wall which formed the boundary on that side of the garden of Devonshire House.

There, set amongst the lilac and syringa bushes, was an arbour in which was placed a wooden seat made comfortable by cushions.

Here there was a little light furnished by a ship's lantern containing a candle, which gave it an intimate atmosphere, and those who occupied the arbour could not be seen from outside. ·

Ilouka sat down on the seat and the Earl in his characteristic manner half-turned to face her.

"What has upset you?" he asked.

"Lord... Marlowe! He has just arrived... and I saw him... I am so... afraid he will... recognise me."

The Earl frowned and said almost as if he spoke to himself:

"I did not anticipate that Marlowe would be here at Devonshire House."

"He is!" Ilouka cried. "Please... you must tell me what I am to... do. Shall I do... or shall I just... stay here in the garden until Mama is ready to leave?"

"That would certainly invite comment," the Earl replied, "and it is doubtful if anybody would believe you were alone."

"Then... what can I do?" Ilouka asked. "and this... may not be the... only Ball at which I shall... see him."

"It is certainly unfortunate that it should happen tonight," the Earl said.

"Even if it were not tonight, it will be another night," Ilouka replied desperately.

There was a little pause before she added:

"Perhaps I had better tell Mama, but I know it will... upset her... and my step-father, who has been so very kind to me, will also be... horrified."

"You should have anticipated that this might happen."

"I know now that I should have done so... but as I explained to you this morning, I was only thinking that it would be... unkind to refuse to help Mr. Archer, and it never entered my head that I might meet... elsewhere any of the... gentlemen you had to... stay."

There was silence, then because she thought the Earl was not going to help her Ilouka looked up at him and her eyes filled with tears as she said:

"I am ashamed... bitterly ashamed that I was so... stupid, and you despise me... but please tell me... what I can do... there is no-one else I can ask."

She sounded very pathetic, but she thought the Earl's expression as he looked at her was grim.

Because she was so upset, and because she thought he despised her even more than he had before, her tears overflowed and ran down her cheeks.

"You say I despise you," the Earl said at length. "If I do not do so, what would you wish me to feel about you?"

Because she was so distraught, Ilouka told the truth.

"I want you to... admire me and to think I am... intelligent and someone you... like."

There was a perceptible pause before the last word as she almost said "love."

Her voice was choked with tears, and as she fumbled for her handkerchief the Earl put his arms around her and pulled her against him.

"You certainly need somebody to look after you."

Ilouka hid her face against his shoulder.

"There is... no-one who will... help me... but you," she sobbed. "I... I could not... marry one of those stupid... young men."

"Why could you not marry one of them?"

Because he was holding her and she could cry against

him, Ilouka found it so comforting that she could answer him quite naturally.

"I do not . . . love him . . . how could I . . . when I . . ."

She stopped, realising that because for the moment he had seemed impersonal, just someone safe and secure, she had almost betrayed herself.

"What were you going to say?" the Earl asked.

"N-nothing . . . it is not . . . important."

"I think it was," he replied, "and if you lie to me again, Ilouka, I shall be very angry."

"No . . . please . . . do not be . . . angry with me . . . I cannot . . . bear it."

She turned her face up to his as she spoke, and in the light of the lantern he could see her wet eyes, the tears on her cheeks, and the trembling of her lips.

He looked down at her for a long moment.

Then when she was still wordlessly beseeching him not to be angry, he pulled her close against him and his lips came down on hers.

It was what Ilouka had longed for, dreamt of, and prayed for ever since he had first kissed her.

Her heart leapt at the wonder of it and she felt once again her vibrations reaching out towards him and knew they joined with his.

He pulled her closer and still closer, and his kiss became more demanding, more insistent, and very much more possessive.

Then, as the ecstasy she had felt before arose within her, she heard the music that came from her heart and knew that this was love—the love that was life itself!

She thought that if she died at this moment it would not matter because she had known and touched the glory of Heaven.

The Earl kissed her until she felt that once again he had carried her to the top of the snow-capped mountains and there was nothing else in the whole Universe but love.

After what seemed a century of time he raised his head and Ilouka said incoherently:

"I . . . I love you! How can a kiss be so . . . wonderful when you . . . do not . . . love me?"

The Earl did not answer, he merely kissed her again.

Then—it seemed much later—when he looked at her Ilouka's eyes were shining like stars, her lips were red from his kisses, and there was a radiance in her face which was as if he had lit a light within her.

As she looked up at him, he could see the love in her eyes.

"I did not mean this to happen tonight," he said.

"I . . . know, but now you have . . . kissed me . . . nothing matters . . . not even . . . Lord Marlowe."

There was just a little tremor in her voice as she spoke his name.

"Unfortunately, he is still a menace," the Earl answered, "and as I have already said, somebody had to look after you, so I suppose it will have to be me!"

"That is what I . . . want you to do . . . but how?"

"As your sins have caught up with you, you must expect to be punished for them."

Ilouka drew in her breath, and because she was a little frightened by what he had said, she moved nearer to him.

"How . . . shall I be . . . punished?"

"Because Lord Marlowe, and perhaps other men from my party, will recognise you," the Earl said, "you will have to go away."

Ilouka stiffened and asked:

"But . . . how can I . . . and where can I . . . go?"

"If I am to help you, it will have to be with me."

Ilouka looked at him, not understanding what he was saying.

Then it flashed through her mind that he was making the same suggestion to her as he had at Lavenham.

The Earl read her thoughts and smiled.

"Yes, I am offering you my protection, but on a rather more permanent basis, as my—wife!"

For a moment Ilouka felt that she could not have heard him aright. Then she said, and her voice trembled:

"Are you . . . asking me to . . . marry you?"

"Can I do anything else?" the Earl enquired. "I have certainly compromised you when you slept in the room next to mine, and I carried you to bed when you were wearing nothing but a nightgown."

Ilouka gave an inarticulate little murmur, and as the colour rose in her cheeks she hid her face against the Earl's shoulder.

"I did not ... mean that to ... happen," she whispered.

"But I did!" the Earl replied. "I wanted you, and I meant you to be mine."

Ilouka raised her head to look at him in astonishment.

"I have just ... realised that was ... why you ... changed my bedroom."

"Of course it was."

He held her closer to him.

"Oh, my darling, you behaved so abominably that I am appalled! It terrified me to think what might have happened to you."

"And yet ... you are still ready to ... marry me?"

"I love you!"

Ilouka gave a little gasp.

"You love ... me ... you really love ... me?"

"I adore you."

"I cannot ... believe it ... I love you so overwhelmingly ... but I never ... thought you would love me."

"It will take me a long time to tell you how much."

"Tell me ... please ... please ... tell me."

"I did not mean to tell you so as quickly as this, but unless you are to have a very dubious reputation, which is something I cannot tolerate in my wife, we will have to use our brains and certainly not allow Marlowe, or anybody else who was at Lavenham, to recognise you."

"How are we to ... prevent them from ... doing that?" Ilouka asked in a small voice.

"By going away," he answered, "and as it happens, I have a very good excuse for doing so."

Ilouka looked at him questioningly.

"Only today I was asked by the Foreign Secretary to

make an unofficial but important diplomatic visit to
several countries in the Mediterranean, even as far as
Turkey and Egypt. I was considering whether or not I
should accept. But I think I might find the journey
tolerably interesting if I took my wife with me on our
honeymoon."

Ilouka gave a little cry.

"Can we do that? Do you really . . . mean you
will . . . take me with . . . you?"

The radiance in her face seemed to light the whole
arbour, then she said in a different tone:

"Are you . . . sure you really want to . . . marry me? I
could not . . . bear you to do so unless you . . . really
wanted me."

The Earl gave a little laugh.

"I have never asked another woman to marry me, but
I want you with me and I do not intend to lose you!"

As he spoke he pulled her roughly against him and
kissed her differently from the way he had before.

Now his lips were fierce, passionate, and demanding,
and Ilouka felt the fire on them and knew as she did so
that a little flame flickered within herself.

It joined with the ecstasy that he always aroused in
her to make it so intense that it was almost a physical
pain.

"I love you . . . I have loved you . . . ever since you
first . . . kissed me," she said, "but I cannot . . . believe
you really . . . love me."

"I will make you believe me," the Earl answered.
"But, my naughty one, we still have to get ourselves
out of the very uncomfortable situation into which your
disgraceful behaviour has landed us."

"I am sorry . . . very sorry," Ilouka said. "Can you
ever . . . forgive me?"

"I suppose I shall have to," he answered, "because if
you had not come to my house it is doubtful that I
should ever have met you."

He paused, then he said:

"No, I am sure that is not true. I believe it was fate

that we should meet, and when I watched you dance I knew you were what I had been looking for all my life, although I had not been aware of it."

"You . . . love . . . me?" Ilouka asked.

"I felt as if you were reaching out to me from the moment you began singing," the Earl said, "and something within me, which I had never known existed before, responded."

"I *was* reaching out towards you," Ilouka said, "and when I danced, I was . . . dancing just for . . . you."

She paused before she added shyly:

"And when you . . . kissed me I felt as if you . . . carried me to the top of the snow-capped mountains and we . . . left the world . . . behind."

"That is exactly what we will do."

There was a deep note in his voice.

Ilouka thought he would kiss her again and she lifted her lips, but instead he moved his mouth along the line of her chin and then went lower to kiss the softness of her neck.

It gave her a strange feeling of excitement which was different from what she had felt before, and she thought that little flames were running through her breasts and up into her throat.

"I love . . . you," she said, but her voice was only a whisper and her breath came quickly in little gasps.

The Earl looked at her and there was a fire in his eyes.

"You are so ridiculously, absurdly beautiful," he said unsteadily, "and unbelievably innocent, I have so much to teach you."

"About . . . what?"

"Love, my darling, and it will be very exciting for me."

"And . . . for . . . me!"

He held her lips captive and she felt as if she gave him not only her heart but her soul and her body.

When it was almost impossible to breathe, with what

she knew was an effort he released her, but she was aware that his heart was beating as frantically as hers.

"Now listen to me, my precious," he said. "We have to be sensible. Yet all I want to do is to kiss you, and go on kissing you for the rest of the night."

"I would . . . love that."

"It is what we will do when we are married," the Earl said, "but now we have to be intelligent, and I need you to help me make a plan to ensure that Lord Marlowe will not hurt us and that your mother and step-father will not be suspicious."

Ilouka gave a sigh of happiness, put her head against his shoulder, and asked:

"What can we . . . do?"

"First of all," the Earl replied, "have you any other names besides Ilouka, which is not only unforgettable to anyone who hears it, but so unusual as to cause comment."

"I was christened 'Mary Nadine Ilouka.'"

"I like Nadine, it suits you," the Earl said, "and we must somehow convince your mother that as I prefer that name it is what you will be known as in future."

He smiled and kissed her forehead as he said:

"But to me you will always be Ilouka, which, although you did not tell me so, means 'She who gives life.'"

"H-how did you . . . discover that?"

"From a friend who speaks Hungarian," the Earl answered, "and it is what you have given me, my lovely one—a new life—a life which is different from what I have known before. But for the moment the Social World must know you as Nadine."

"Then what . . . must we do?"

"I will accept the Foreign Secretary's proposition. We will be married immediately, but in the country with nobody there except for your parents and one of my special friends who was not staying with me when I was entertaining a very beautiful, very naughty little dancer."

"All I . . . want is to be your . . . wife."

"That is what you will be," the Earl promised, "and one thing is very certain, my alluring, adorable Ilouka, never again will you do anything so outrageous as to dance for any man except me, and never in any circumstances will you pretend to be an actress."

Ilouka looked at him to see if he was angry, but his eyes were twinkling and there was a smile on his lips.

"I love you! I love you!" she cried. "I will do exactly what you want me to do, and I promise you I will be very... very good for ever... and ever."

The Earl laughed.

"I very much doubt it," he said. "At the same time, my darling, we have a great deal to discover about ourselves, and although our hearts know already that we belong to each other, there are other things I want to learn about you."

"As I want to know everything about you," Ilouka added, "and of course to meet Apollo."

The Earl laughed again.

He held her close to him and kissed her fiercely and passionately until the arbour and the garden vanished and the music they could hear was not from the Band in the distance but from their hearts.

Then he was carrying her up into the starlit sky, above the snow-capped mountains into a Heaven where there was only the love which came from the life pulsating within them.

That was theirs for Eternity.

ABOUT THE AUTHOR

BARBARA CARTLAND is the bestselling authoress in the world, according to the *Guinness Book of World Records*. She has sold over 200 million books and has beaten the world record for five years running, last year with 24 and the previous years with 24, 20, and 23.

She is also an historian, playwright, lecturer, political speaker and television personality, and has now written over 320 books.

She has also had many historical works published and has written four autobiographies as well as the biographies of her mother and that of her brother, Ronald Cartland, who was the first Member of Parliament to be killed in the last war. This book has a preface by Sir Winston Churchill and has just been republished with an introduction by Sir Arthur Bryant.

Love at the Helm, a novel written with the help and inspiration of the late Earl Mountbatten of Burma, Uncle of His Royal Highness Prince Philip, is being sold for the Mountbatten Memorial Trust.

In 1978 Miss Cartland sang an Album of Love Songs with the Royal Philharmonic Orchestra.

She is unique in that she was #1 and #2 in the Dalton List of Bestsellers, and one week had four books in the top twenty.

In private life Barbara Cartland, who is a Dame of the Order of St. John of Jerusalem, Chairman of the St. John Council in Hertfordshire and Deputy President of the St. John Ambulance Brigade, has also fought for better conditions and salaries for midwives and nurses.

As President of the Royal College of Midwives (Hertfordshire Branch) she has been invested with the first badge of Office ever given in Great Britain, which was subscribed to by the midwives themselves.

Barbara Cartland is deeply interested in vitamin therapy and is President of the British National Association for Health. Her book, *The Magic of Honey*, has sold throughout the world and is translated into many languages.

She has a magazine "Barbara Cartland's World of Romance" now being published in the USA.

Barbara Cartland

The world's bestselling author of romantic fiction. Her stories are always captivating tales of intrigue, adventure and love.

☐	20235	LOVE WINS	$1.95
☐	20505	SECRET HARBOR	$1.95
☐	20234	SHAFT OF SUNLIGHT	$1.95
☐	20014	GIFT OF THE GODS	$1.95
☐	20126	AN INNOCENT IN RUSSIA	$1.95
☐	20013	RIVER OF LOVE	$1.95
☐	14503	THE LIONESS AND THE LILY	$1.75
☐	14133	THE PRUDE AND THE PRODIGAL	$1.75
☐	13032	PRIDE AND THE POOR PRINCESS	$1.75
☐	13984	LOVE FOR SALE	$1.75
☐	14248	THE GODDESS AND THE GAIETY GIRL	$1.75
☐	14360	SIGNPOST TO LOVE	$1.75
☐	14361	FROM HELL TO HEAVEN	$1.75
☐	13985	LOST LAUGHTER	$1.75
☐	22513	MUSIC FROM THE HEART	$1.95
☐	14902	WINGED MAGIC	$1.95
☐	14922	A PORTRAIT OF LOVE	$1.95